Cappuccino for Callie

Also by Melanie Greene

Pier 3 Coffee Series

Mocha for Mateo *(Alicia & Mateo)*

Cappuccino for Callie *(Abraham & Callie)*

Latte for Leyla *(Austin & Leyla)*

Roll of the Dice Series

Rocket Man *(Serena & Dillon)*

Ready to Roll *(Janice & Miguel)*

Eye of the Tiger *(Natalie & Evan)*

Let the Good Times Roll *(Chloe & Gabriel)*

Roll of a Lifetime *(Rachel & Theo)*

Roll Play *(Kim-ly & Tómas)*

On a Roll *(Gillian & Vic)*

Roll in the Hay *(Anton & Cisco) - available to subscribers or as a
bonus in the Roll of the Dice novella anthology*

Other Contemporary Romances

Retreat to Love *(Ashlyn & Caleb)*

Feather in Her Cap *(Jeannie & Brendan)*

Twelve Scorching Days *(Sarita & Scorch)*

Margo of the Bells (Margo & Karl)

Curiosity (Amity & Josh) - story in the It's Always Been You anthology

Cappuccino for Callie

MELANIE GREENE

Because it's my 12th book
And because he fills my life with song
This one is for Kieran

Chapter One

Callie Hamasaki batted at the window blind cords as she passed, having given up on finding a way to angle them that properly diffused the light in her temporary apartment. Every single window faced west, the ocean views trying to calm her like they weren't the latest problem piling onto the stress of her life.

No matter how she framed it, she was smack in the midst of a disaster. Another epic loss, in a life fractured by epic losses, both material and social. If only she knew how to guarantee that, this time, she wouldn't have to go through any extra levels of hardship before her triumphant success.

Been there, done that, overcame it all.

And she would overcome again. Triumphant, overarching success, that was the game plan. Just as soon as she grappled this apartment into some kind of usable order.

She paced the perimeter of the rooms she'd sublet from her college roommate, Alicia. Maybe to an outsider she'd look like a leopard cat restlessly testing the limits of a new cage, but she couldn't settle in until she got to know the space, feeling out its dark corners and deceptive shadows. Learning the light:

that essential first step to using a space as the home base for her art.

Callie always claimed she could paint anywhere, but made that claim without including her caveats about natural and artificial lights, ventilation, or storage. All the things she'd balanced so perfectly in her studio in Monterey—until it went up in literal smoke, leaving her with a coveted contract for a solo exhibition and a stack of completed canvases now curdled to burnt blackness.

The damn fire had blazed through Callie's building right when Alicia was moving in with her partner, Mateo. When she told her friend about the dim and dismal extended-stay motel Callie's renter's insurance hooked her up with, she offered up her place in Surfside, a few hours north of Monterey. Callie knew the town from her college days, and was more than glad to return to it, leaving the smoking rubble of her old life behind.

Alicia left a decent stash of furniture in the apartment for her, which helped. Callie had salvaged barely enough from the ashy ruins to fill her little van for the drive up the California coastline. But before she hauled in the remains of her possessions, she needed to grasp what it would take to turn the place into her perfect creative haven.

So, she paced.

It wasn't what she'd have picked for herself if she'd had the whole world and plenty of time to search. Not only did the windows face west, many were sunk under a balcony overhang. The ceiling fixture in the living room was a track light. The space-saving sink and shower in the bathroom would cramp her clean-up process. And the tiny closet made her slightly grateful that the restorers deemed most of her wardrobe too scorched to salvage.

But she hadn't had time to be picky. Her options were the dingy motel, her childhood bedroom and whatever space she could claim in her parents' garage for painting, or Alicia's sublet. And at least the sublet, for all its flaws, gave her the chance to use every inch of its sub-par space to work towards the triumph she refused to put off, no matter what it took out of her.

Abraham Wells removed two water bottles from his fridge, replacing them with the two he'd just taken from the dishwasher and refilled. He stashed the cool bottles in the side pockets of his blue backpack and headed to the door.

His brother glanced up from his video game. "Where are you off to? Hiking?"

He shook his head. "Caving."

Austin crinkled his brow. "Thought caving was the green backpack."

"Green for hiking. Blue for caving."

He probably didn't sound as annoyed as he felt after correcting his brother for the six-hundredth time, since Austin grinned and said, "And red for when you have a hot date and may not show up until morning."

He sounded, as always, entirely too amused by his brother's systems. Abraham told himself he didn't care if his family wanted to laugh at him for having color-coded backpacks depending on what activity he was up to. It was fine. Let them laugh. Let them giggle. Let them go to goddamn hell.

He didn't want to change the specifics of his life. It was better for his mental load when he set aside time to organize in advance, so he didn't have to figure shit out when he was on the way out the door. So, yeah, his backpacks were always set for him to grab and go. His car's tank was rarely below half-full. He did his laundry when he was down to four pairs of clean boxers. He couldn't prepare for every eventuality in life, but he could do sensible things to make everyday life smoother.

He rolled his eyes at Austin, who was already engrossed back in his game. Escaping out of the apartment, he reviewed the route he wanted to take. He hadn't been to the Addax cave system in a few months. He was thinking of following the green slope pathway he'd discussed with a caving friend recently. It meant navigating from the more northerly entrance, which wasn't his fave. Too much brush to wriggle past. But once he made it past the portal, it would open up to a series of walkable caverns before he branched off to explore the green slopes themselves.

Set on working through the steps, Abraham nearly plowed into a veritable carnival of nonsense filling the foyer.

He'd grown up in this apartment building his parents owned. It was hardly the first time he'd encountered people moving piles of stuff into the place. But there was something unusually motley and festive and intrusive about this crowd.

It was easy to peg them as a group of friends, rather than professional movers, even without blanket wrapped furnishings or neatly taped and labeled boxes. The stuff they carried existed in some space between move-in day and housewarming party: a paint-splashed box full of incomprehensible wood pieces, tote bags of groceries, two crates full of bottles and jars. Bundles of cloth trailing from the arms of a couple of conspiratorially laughing guys.

One of the cloth bearers reached over to snag his arm as he moved past. "Hold up, you live here?"

Abraham just looked at him, which didn't deter the guy from letting out a piercing whistle to get everyone's attention.

"Hey, everybody. Hang on. This guy is gonna help us."

Well, that was taking quite a lot for granted. But all the goddam customer service training he'd done since he and his siblings opened Pier Three Coffee kicked in. Plus, if his parents or brother heard about him being rude to visitors, they'd stack that little nugget atop the pile of evidence they'd collected that Abraham was ... Well, whatever they thought about him. That he couldn't take things in stride. That it was their job to reform the world to ease his navigation through it. Some kind of judgment they would never ever speak, but which would always lurk behind their eyes.

He used the pretense of hitching up his backpack to detach himself from the guy. "What can I do?" He scanned the various loads they were carrying, searching for anything so unwieldy it was about to topple.

Cloth bundle guy seemed to guess what he was doing and shook his head. "We've got this stuff."

"But no one remembers where our friend's staying. I know it's in this building," said one of the crate-bearing women. Her tone was more than a touch impatient.

"I believe you," cloth bundle guy told her, not quite sincerely. "But what apartment?"

Crate woman pushed a puff of air out of her cheeks. "She's not answering her texts."

Abraham stepped in before they could launch further into some kind of bickering routine that would trap him in the foyer forever. "Who are you looking for?"

The other three people turned away from the crate-cloth battle and spoke at once. "Callie Hamasaki."

It wasn't even how in sync they were that gave him pause. It was the utter reverence when they breathed her name. He didn't know how his sister's friend inspired such awe, but he was sure all that adulation wasn't something he wanted to deal with.

She was two-thirds of the way through shoving Alicia's unwieldy bookcase from the sitting area to the bedroom when someone knocked. Callie scrubbed her dusty hands onto the butt of her shorts and fumbled at the latch of her new front door.

Since she hadn't been expecting anyone, maybe it made sense that she'd be surprised. But something hitched sideways in her when she caught sight of the grumpy, narrowed, deep brown eyes of the man at her threshold.

"Um?"

"You've got visitors."

She didn't know why he sounded so grim and disapproving.

She didn't know who he even was.

And then her arm moved like she was sketching his form, and she noted consciously what her visual processor had already established. The Wells siblings weren't identical, but their cheekbones, their noses, the bow of their lips were all the same. "Oh. You're Abraham."

The grumpy eyes got deeper and narrower. Just a fraction, but it altered his expression from general annoyance, to a specific kind of guardedness aimed squarely at her.

"Yes, I'm the brother with one hand. Austin's the other one. You're Callie. The foyer is full of people claiming you invited them but didn't tell them your apartment number. If you want to see them, go meet them or text them or something."

With that, he turned and strode away.

Callie stood there, agape. The back of her neck burned, but she wasn't going to fluster herself chasing after him to, what, apologize for not recognizing him at first sight? It wasn't in anyone's interests—and certainly not hers—to follow those strong, tanned calves down the hall. He could think insulting things about her if he wanted.

Not that she could sort out how it was insulting, if she had recognized him only because of his congenital limb difference. They really didn't know each other, and she'd never seen him with a beard before. As often as she'd gone with Alicia to her parents' penthouse for dinner or to use their laundry and pool during college, she'd barely encountered either of her friend's brothers; they were pretty much off doing their own thing in those years. Especially the older one, who'd moved away from Surfside for both of his undergrad and post-grad programs.

She shut the door and shook her head. His mood didn't need to be her problem. And apparently, she had people to see.

In the bathroom, she washed up and recovered her phone from the charger. After letting the crew know where she was, she debated and rejected the idea of sending Alicia a question about how to un-piss-off her brother.

What did it matter? He could fuck off if he wanted. She had things to do, and, based on the noise in the corridor, a lot of hugs to dispense.

Chapter Two

Fuck but she was cute.

Abraham hadn't been prepared. Should he have been prepared? It wasn't like he'd never met Callie before. She'd spent a Thanksgiving with them once. Or, Abraham was fairly sure it had been Callie that his sister brought home from college; she was the friend Alicia mentioned most.

Whatever accurate or flawed, faded memories he had leapt off a cliff into oblivion when faced with the reality of the woman standing in the apartment doorway, looking at him like he was an incompetent intruder. The hallway lighting wasn't great—he should tell his brother to check the bulbs—but somehow the shadows managed to play intriguingly over her face, tracing the sweep of her lashes and line of her jaw.

Completely, totally cute.

He didn't have time for cute.

Her people wanted to know where she lived. He knew where she lived. He let her know they were looking for her.

End of story.

Now he could walk right past all their messy loudness—

he'd figured out that the stuff was all to do with painting, once they said who they were looking for—and get on with exploring the Addax caves.

Never mind that he was beset by some subterranean unease springing from her twice damned cuteness. It was like staring out at a day that appeared still and calm, until a tiny yellow butterfly appeared, bouncing and burbling on heretofore invisible air currents.

Callie Hamasaki had no business drawing his attention to how the world was moving around him in ways he preferred not to notice.

Two hours passed as he explored the green slope, twisting his way through some shallow tubes until he emerged from the sandstone and onto the sand and made his way back up the coast to his car. The path had been tricky enough in places that he'd shut out every other thought. No Pier Three bank balances, no accounting problems for his freelance customers. Nothing about his family, or the state of the world, or any particular pair of light brown eyes taking in the contours of his torso.

He'd nearly made it to the refuge of his home when a laughing kind of singing pinned him in place.

Two apartments from his, Callie's front door was open, music twinkling out of it as bright and colorful as all those friends of hers. And of the woman herself as she popped her head round the door, and said, "Abraham, perfect. Come here."

Like whatever she had going on was superior in every way to whatever he had going on.

It was those customer service instincts of his, and not the

way she stretched out the syllables of his name like salt water taffy, that prompted him to obey.

When he'd knocked on her door earlier, he hadn't really gotten a look at the apartment behind her. It had seemed pretty much just like they've left it once he and Austin had helped Alicia move in with Mateo. A sparse selection of furniture—some Alicia's own pieces and some from the basement storage where they stashed anything half decent that was abandoned by their tenants.

But that was before the invasion of an entire caravan's worth of guests. Now she had canvases and easels lined up against the walls. The kitchen counter was covered in food and paints, the sofa draped in drop cloths. She also had two suitcases parked by the bedroom door and a hat tree he was sure he'd have noticed if someone in her parade of art people had been carrying it. The thing was all kinds of bright, even before being covered in scarves and caps.

"You like that?" she asked. She gave it a little shake, so the disco balls attached to the upright sparkled and spun. "It's so whimsical right? My friend Salt—Owen Salt, he was here earlier. He made it for me a few years ago. Luckily it was near my front door in Monterey, so the fire didn't get it like it did most of my furniture."

Abe nodded. A kind thing to do would be to remember that this woman's life had gone up in smoke just a couple of weeks ago. She'd lost her home, and some of her work. Or maybe a lot of her work—Alicia had been suitably dramatic about it all. Callie was going to have to recreate a large number of art pieces. Canvases? He didn't know the terminology.

Point was, she had an exhibition of some sort coming up, and would have to hustle to be ready for it. So, whatever she'd called him in for, he'd help her out.

"It's nice, and ... bright," he said, making like he got the point of the rainbow patterns swirling all up and down it.

He assumed this Salt guy was good enough at art for Callie's praise to be warranted. From what Alicia always claimed, Callie had supernova talent, so probably if she liked something, it was worthwhile.

Well, she hadn't likely called him in to get him to glue little mirrors to her furniture. "Did you need help unpacking, or moving things?"

"What? No, no thanks. I'm pretty much set but ... Alicia told you about my show, right?"

He nodded.

"So, Wolfgang Lewis, that's the gallery owner, he's planning on stopping by when he's on the way to a wedding in a couple of weeks. And I need to get started on pieces from the show. I'm going to—I was going to head into San Jose to pick up supplies later but, Sofia. You saw her earlier, too. She was one of the TAs when I was in college, and she teaches studio work up on campus now. She called up a few of the people who still live around here. And they kind of? I guess they scavenged their studios for supplies for me."

Callie was darting from crate to box to kitchen, pulling together an assortment of things. Every time she moved around him, it was in a different way. Sliding behind him, crossing in front of him, edging up and putting her hand to his shoulder while leaning sideways past him to grab a jar from her bathroom.

Abe got vertigo from standing still and watching her.

"Anyway, I like this afternoon light and I've got these supplies now. It's just about enough to get me started. And you're here so ..." She stopped a few feet from him and looked at him expectantly.

He was too befuddled to prompt her for an answer.

She huffed and grabbed a chair from the dinette set, thumping it down next to the balcony. Then she snagged a stool and set it by the easel.

She propped one of her graceful hands on the curve of her hip, and he swallowed hard.

"Will you model for me, or what?"

Chapter Three

His *face*.

She fought to contain her giggles, lest he furrow that brow even more deeply. "Oh, come on, you're not working today. And you're back from whatever errand you were running."

"Caving," he said, tugging his backpack strap like that explained everything.

She tilted her head. There was a guy in college, he lived down the hall from her and Alicia, who would go on and on about exploring the cave systems in the foothills. She'd always thought it was his excuse to hunt for magic mushrooms. But maybe there really were caves to explore around Surfside.

Or maybe Abraham had been off eating mushrooms. Either way, he was with her now, and now is when she needed a model.

"Come on, I ran into your brother earlier, he said you weren't busy. I'm not gonna steal your soul. I just want you to sit there and stare out the window for a bit."

She wasn't defining how long 'a bit' was. She had the feeling that if she gave him an estimate, he would set a count-down timer. Still, he wasn't complying.

"Abraham. It's not exactly difficult. You literally will be sitting down. I can even change the music if you like."

"Music's fine," he grunted.

She stifled her laugh at hearing somebody actually grunt words. This grumpy taciturn thing of his was too adorable. Maybe someone else would rethink playing with him like she was, but after decades of working with live models, Callie found they fell into line better for her if she was lighthearted and didn't treat sitting like it was some huge serious thing.

She deliberately ignored him for a minute, lining up the beauteous new Rosemary & Co. brushes Sofia had gifted her, and squeezing out the oils she needed on the flimsy plastic palette Amity'd handed over with a shrug. She'd apologized for not having better stuff she could contribute to the surprise supply party they'd thrown her that morning.

She wasn't complaining. Even though the palette was objectively a piece of beginner-level crap. Amity and them had shown up all super complimentary and sympathetic— and generous with both praise and possessions. Sofia had hugged her and said everyone at the art department was excited she was in town again, and she'd love to have Callie give a guest lecture when she had her exhibition under control.

Considering how much Sofia had pulled out of the art department's summer storage to loan her, Callie should probably take that request seriously. Later.

For now, she needed pieces, and she needed them fast. Wolfgang Lewis had already printed up promo for her show, using one of her large form figurative paintings—one that, fortunately, she'd stashed at her parents' place after she took it up to Berkeley so her favorite photographer could capture it. She needed to recreate that feel, so he could continue to build publicity for her. "Not facsimiles," he'd messaged her. "But that same vibe. We can use the story of the fire, and images of the lost pieces from your website and social media to create buzz."

Because that's what having a whole goddamn stack of canvases curdle into the most appalling smelling char was: a chance to build buzz.

Whatever.

Callie was a goddamn genius. It was gonna be work. And it was going to take ridiculous hours. But she had the discipline, and she had the talent. She just needed Alicia's brother to plop his ass down in that chair, so she could get on with it. "What are you waiting for?"

"I ..." He shut his mouth without getting any further with that answer, and jutted his chin.

She lunged forward and snagged the sleeve of his shirt, tugging him towards the chair. "If you really had a problem, you'd have left by now. You didn't, so that means you can do this."

She slipped the backpack off his shoulder and remembered to set it down instead of dropping it, lest she crush his stash of hallucinogenic fungi, or whatever he had packed in there. She noticed his water bottles were empty, so she took one to refill it while she went to retrieve a cleaning rag and a mug for solvent from the kitchen.

Abraham was examining her easel and set up, but as she approached, he moved to his chair and finally sat.

She considered and rejected the idea of patting his shoulder in praise. "Here you go. Oh, and take your shirt off."

Abraham half rose, but she didn't back away from him, so he sank back into his sliver of personal space. "What?"

"Your shirt. The whole point is for you to sit in this window so your torso is half lit and half shadowed. Don't worry, it's not creepy. I'm not oiling up your chest or stripping off your pants."

His hand moved protectively over his fly. He quickly

jerked it away, scratching at his chest instead. "Okay?" He did that grumpy throat clearing thing again.

"You don't have to tell anyone you posed, if you're shy about being represented. Even though you should be super honored to be featured in a Callie Hamasaki original."

"I think people might just figure out that the painting of the one armed man is of me." Amusing, how being irked and suspicious got him to finally utter several words in a row.

She scoffed. "I'm not painting your limbs, just your torso. Torso, neck, head. It's all about composition and the balance between fleeting and eternal beauty. Didn't you see any of my studies? I know Alicia values me for my stellar friendship and not for me being a phenomenal talent, but surely she's showed you my site before?"

He wasn't stripping off, so she figured he wasn't yet convinced.

"Come on, sun's burning."

Abraham plucked at the neck of his tee. "I've been caving."

"Yeah?"

"So now I stink."

"Oh, you stink. Oh, dearie me." She stepped back. "Dude. I'll be nose-deep in oil paints and supposedly odorless solvent. I'm not going to collapse from the pure virility of your unfettered manly musk."

His eyes. How did they keep getting so deep? She snagged one of the Strathmore newsprint pads Salt had left her and sketched the way his brow furrowed down over his thick lashes. When she looked up for another glimpse at the angle of his cheekbones, she saw he'd finally shed his tee and was staring out towards the stretch of Pacific Ocean visible from her balcony. He sat as if he could transport himself onto the distantly crashing waves, if he just thought hard enough about not being exactly where she wanted him.

At one point on the green slope he'd been belly crawling through a twisty narrow tunnel that emerged into a flowstone cavern whose floor was a good four feet drop below him. He'd had to dig in with his toes to regain his balance and keep himself from dropping headfirst onto the stone. Then there'd been a fun few minutes of wedging himself onto his left shoulder until he could free his arm into the room in search of a handhold secure enough to stop him from smacking his noggin on limestone.

He'd gotten clear, of course. The point wasn't that he'd gotten clear.

It was that even after he emerged, and removed his helmet and headlamp, and dusted down his clothes, he'd still been real up close and personal with what could only be called cave slime. Plus, he'd bruised his shoulder and scraped his calf, and generally felt like he was better off in the shower than in Callie's apartment. No matter how true it was that the rest of his day was free.

The woman apparently wasn't bothered by the sweat tracks down his face and what he was sure was a distinct dirt line were his T-shirt met his biceps.

"What's your call? You posing, or not?"

She needed them to not waste the sun. For him to just sit around with his hand in shadow and his stump lit up bright.

Well, she was the artist.

So, he sat. And sat. And sat. Finally, he glanced at her, but she was intent on doing something with a little knife thing and those tubes of paint colors.

So, he kept sitting.

She was singing along to her playlist as she worked. He'd have guessed it was K-pop, but maybe it was something Japanese instead. He didn't know if she spoke Korean. Of course, from what he gathered a lot of people sang K-pop phonetically. So he could stop all of his speculations and assumptions. He did remember Alicia saying something about how she lived in Japan her first few years. Why would he remember that, but not the practically translucent glow of Callie's skin? Or the way she so effortlessly arranged her space so her every movement while working was fluid and competent? Or the birthmark peeking out just past the swing of her hair when she shook it back?

Seemed like that would be the kind of thing he would remember for years, even if he wasn't paying too much attention to Alicia and her friends during college.

And now he was thinking about how to avoid thinking about how dynamic and magnetic Callie was, which was worse than letting his brain wander around admiring everything about her.

He got a respite when he heard someone knocking in the hallway. "Son? Abraham?"

He flinched and Callie practically pounced on him. "Is that your mom?"

It was. And it was no good pretending otherwise.

"Katherine," she called. "We're in here." Callie gave a gleeful little bounce.

Like a moth to Callie's flame, his mom came straight into them.

"Oh my, Callie. Look at you. Hello, sweet girl." She bestowed kisses before turning to raise an eyebrow his way. "I was looking for my son. But I didn't expect I'd find quite so much of him."

He scrubbed his hand over his face. "Hi, Mom."

"Don't get too excited, Katherine, but I'm about to make your son into a world famous muse for the ages." Callie pointed one of her five or six paintbrushes at him.

"Oh, how fun. Can I see?"

She waggled the brush towards his mom. "All will be revealed."

He cleared his throat. "Were you looking for me, Mom?"

"Right. Yes, I was heading down to meet my friends for lunch and I started having some vasomotor symptoms. I figured you'd have a bottle of water I could borrow, because I'm definitely having wine with lunch. And you know that means it'll just get worse this afternoon."

"Vaso-what? Are you okay?" Callie looked at him. "You didn't tell me your mom wasn't—"

He shook his head. "She's in menopause."

"Perimenopause," Mom corrected.

"She is in perimenopause," he said, carefully. "Part of that involves vasomotor impacts, such as hot flashes. There's no easy way to combat them. But staying hydrated helps."

Now Callie was definitely holding back giggles at his expense.

"We're all about breaking the barrier of silence about our bodily processes and normalizing the discussion of medical issues," he recited in a monotone.

Callie bounced more with glee.

"Speaking of issues," Mom asked, "are you normally this funky smelling? Do you need to see a dermatologist?"

He was torn between flinging himself off the balcony and crawling under the chair. While he debated the two, Callie thought to jump in with an explanation of how she stopped him from showering because she needed his body in that chair with no delay.

He reached for his backpack and fished out his keys. "There's cold water in the fridge," he told Mom, who took them but made no move to wrap up her chat with Callie about her move up to Surfside.

"Will you not be late for lunch?" he finally asked, which earned him matching reproving looks from the women. Mom did wrap Callie in a hug, apologizing for her sheen of peri-menopausal sweat, and went off to grab one of his water bottles.

Callie was back fussing at her easel when Mom returned his keys, but he had no expectation that the subject was dropped. It wasn't a minute later before she turned to him to say, "I love your mom. She is the absolute best."

Now he knew Callie didn't direct all of her hyperbolic praise only to herself. That was something. He told himself he didn't care why his half-hearted grunt made her giggle. She seemed to be working with more fervor, so giggling had to be a good sign of progress. And the more she progressed, the sooner she'd be finished with him. And the sooner he could get back to all the nothing he had planned for the rest of the day.

Not that she was counting, but it wasn't until four days after Abraham had snatched up his shirt and backpack and fled her apartment that she saw him again.

She finally felt organized enough to get out and explore Surfside a little bit, and was meeting Alicia at her and her brothers' coffee shop before heading to San Jose to pick up the order she'd called in to her favorite art supply store. This whole insurance settlement thing was a tangle of knotted yarn she'd never find the end of, but at least she'd had the contract from The Wolfgang Lewis Gallery to establish the worth of her destroyed pieces. It gave her a jump start on replacing her studio setup with high quality items.

Pier Three Coffee was looking good, if she did say so herself. Back when the siblings had first gone into business, and were converting it from a bait shop to a coffee shop, she'd driven up a couple of times to work with Alicia and Austin on the redesign. Looking back, she wondered why she hadn't run into Abraham on those visits, but Austin was the one who had construction experience. And Alicia was her bestie. So maybe he'd been around, acting his usual silent self, while she and

Alicia talked and Austin filled the available space with his court jester routine.

They'd made minor changes to the place since opening, but her original design for the interior was still the strong scaffolding through which people encountered the cafe. The retro pastry display case up against the modern poured concrete surface counter. The floating shelves for cups and supplies behind the baristas. The mismatched chairs and tables in complementary sunset hues against the midday-summer-blue of the walls. And the wide windows and sliding glass doors onto the patio overlooking the Pacific. Everything was comfortable, welcoming and energizing, just as she'd planned when Alicia first articulated her vision for the place.

And there was her friend, stripping off her apron and coming around the counter to give her a giant hug.

They separated, pulling each other towards a corner seating area, already talking over each other about Alicia's haircut and Callie's new top, and the wonky window in Callie's new bedroom, and whether or not she was free to join their crowd on the beach for a Friday night bonfire. "We do it most weeks," Alicia said. "Early, to catch the sunset, and because most of us have morning shifts."

"I knew it. You fell for Mateo because he's a baker."

"Stop. I thought I knew what morning shifts were until I got with that man. He's lucky he's so cute."

"He's the lucky one." Callie meant it entirely.

Alicia's face bloomed with a dreamy smile. "Hmm."

"And you know, it makes sense."

"What does?"

"This whole being madly in love thing of yours. I wasn't sure I got it before, but now ..."

Alicia laughed "You barely even met him."

"No, I know. It's not Mateo, though I'm sure his buns are as tasty as you say."

Alicia snorted.

Callie stuck out her tongue, but then got serious. "I don't think you were really … ready for a while. Not settled enough in here." Her palm traced little circles over her heart. "Partly from the bullshit at your old job. But—I don't know. It's like you've been growing into this more firmly defined sense of yourself than you were, going back to college, at least. Maybe from the process of establishing and growing Pier Three, or maybe just a function of life. Anyway, you are this total exemplar of who you are now. You're a thousand percent Alicia. It seems like that kind of opened up the opportunity for you to bloom into a woman who's madly in love."

Callie smirked, shedding some of the gravitas. "Just your bad luck that you became all open to love at the same time that you were banging the baker."

"Oh, ha ha. If you're so wise about humanity now, explain to me how you've been ten thousand percent yourself practically since birth, but you haven't gotten all goofy in love like me? If your theory is true—not that I'm saying I haven't always been a thousand percent myself—you should have shacked up with Franklin, or Shigeru, or … who was that guy with the?" Alicia mimed large ears.

"Caden Miller." Callie grimaced. "We don't talk about Caden Miller."

Alicia was laughing and scrolling through her phone. "No, but look. Your dream man, Callie. The guy was perfect. And I don't even mean the ears, because what he chose to do to them was his own business." She flashed Callie a look at his Insta profile.

"You are the absolute worst."

"Come on, check this. Here he is eating charcoal ice cream with huckleberry sauce. And have you even seen how well his ska band is doing? It's an inspiration," she sing-songed, though fortunately not in a ska style.

Callie snatched her phone away and turned off the screen. "Fine. I concede. It takes more than being a thousand percent yourself to end up as smugly in love as you and Mateo are. You found the confluence of your own identity and the perfect man, who is also, I presume, somewhere near that thousand percent mark himself. Shigeru and all those guys—Caden Miller included—weren't ever going to be candidates because they didn't have the completeness to match my own perfection."

She pretended to buff her paint-flecked nails. Alicia faux-buffed her own. "I'll accept that theory."

"As we can clearly see, I am so stellar that it will take somebody pretty fucking perfect to keep up with me." And Callie absolutely, a thousand percent, did not fight down an accelerated pulse or work too hard to appear casual about the timing when Abraham chose that moment to appear in front of them.

He didn't precisely plan to interact with his sister and her friend. It was just that he knew Alicia liked a chai in the afternoons. So, when he saw her taking a break, he decided to make her one. It was hardly the first time he'd done it.

And it would be rude to bring something to Alicia, but not to Callie. Abe wasn't rude.

He set the tray down between them, gesturing for Alicia to take hers before tapping his finger on the lid of another drink. "It's a vanilla cappuccino with oat milk. I wasn't sure if you do dairy or not."

She reached out tentatively, and he felt a flash of disquiet based solely on the fact that when she'd been painting—and when saying apparently hilarious things to Alicia—she'd displayed all these quicksilver movements. Now her head was stacked high above her spine, gaze darting between him and the drink like it might be a trap.

"I do drink milk," she said. "But, thank you." She didn't sound so sure about those thanks.

To his vast irritation, Alicia was watching him like he had thoughts her narrowed eyes could yank out of his head. He absolutely did not have any thoughts.

He'd brought her drinks before, without her acting like he had thoughts she should invade. "What's that one?" she asked, tapping the lid of the third drink.

"Nothing," he said, reaching to slide it towards himself. "Ruthie got in early, so I'm taking my break, is all."

Alicia was full on doing the thing she called laser eyes now, where she acted like she was in charge of how her brothers should get on with their lives. He lasered his right back at her, then cursed himself for it. The silent interaction made him miss whatever expression Callie made when she tasted the drink he'd brought her.

"It's super yum," she said, her voice that happy lilt again. But how could he tell if she meant it, or if she was doing her usual overblown praise thing?

And how did he already know her enough to have opinions about the way she spoke?

One thing was sure, he wasn't the kind of guy that would pass her thousand percent perfect test. He was too full of rules for himself and too tied to his routines and too ignorant about things like art and culture to fit in with a crowd like the ones who'd brought her all the art supplies.

So when Callie bestowed a grin on him and said, "If you're on break you should join us," he knew it was the right move to decline with thanks, grab his cortado, and banish himself to the patio, alone.

Chapter Five

He wasn't done contemplating the incoming tide when Austin rounded the side of the building and vaulted himself onto the bench opposite him.

"Where's Alicia?"

Abe's shrug wasn't enough of an answer for the brat, who stood to scan the interior of the cafe. He opted not to tell him that she and Callie were seated on the corner sofa and therefore unlikely to be visible from the picnic bench he'd chosen.

Not that he'd specifically chosen to sit there to be out of their view, or vice versa.

Austin plopped back down and drummed his hands on the table. "Never mind, I'll catch her later. But, hey, you're going to flip. Listen."

Abe glanced at him. Austin's opinion about things that would make him flip rarely met the definition.

"No, for real this time. I just came down from the studios."

A couple months back, their landlady let them know she was selling the building so she could retire to where her daughter and grandkids lived. They hadn't been able to secure the funding to buy it off Mrs. Vallejo outright, thanks to some lean years of recession and their determination to keep their employees at a living wage even when it cut into the fund they'd been growing specifically to buy the building.

As a last-ditch effort, Austin came up with a plan to convert Alicia's apartment above the café into a meeting suite with recording studios for people who wanted to work remotely, but not always in their homes or the busy café environment. He'd set up soundproof studios for podcasters and the like, complete with mics and mixing equipment that was fancier than most people would spring for on their own. Abe and Alicia had been skeptical, but Austin contracted with a local employee services company willing to fund the build out in order to guarantee themselves space for weekly meetings, in lieu of renting an entire office suite for a team that preferred to avoid the office.

"So the Vallejo's had this employee, Cesar Santos. Do you remember him?"

Why would he remember some guy who worked for the bait shop before they acquired it? He'd never been into fishing, unlike Austin, who took to it the same way he took to anything that required fiddly nonsense. Untangling lines, tying lures, all that stuff.

Austin knew better than to wait for his answer. "Anyway, point is, Mr. Santos. His son and daughter have been fishing since they were kids. These days, they've gotten involved with this collective of sports fishermen who have, like, newsletters about fishing gear and posts about tournaments and that kind of thing. And one of their projects is a family of podcasts, as these groups are called. So. Diana and Isaac Santos, they've been putting out a podcast about fishing for a while now. And this collective is hiring them to engineer all their sound—the people with quality info aren't always the best at packaging it to keep subscribers. They love the nostalgia factor of working from our studios, you know—the building where they learned so much about the sport to start with. Plus, it's convenient since they're still locals. So ..."

Austin's restlessly tapping hands accelerated into a proper drum roll.

"The Norbay Podcast Network is officially contracted to produce and engineer out of Pier Three Studios, Surfside, California. Imagine that going out into the ears of every sport fishing enthusiast that subscribes to their stuff."

Abe's eyes cut to the waves again, contemplating this vision. He wasn't a podcast guy himself—Abe preferred quiet solitude. But it was obvious from their market research that he wasn't in the majority there.

"And bonus, too, since so many of our other studio users aren't exactly morning people. Isaac and Diana are totally up at dawn types—we should get them to join us at bonfire. They contracted for fifteen hours a week, but it's all six to nine a.m. Leaves us with tons of hours left to rent out the booths to other users. Win, win, and win."

"How long is the contract for?" Abe was running numbers in his head.

"I got them to sign for a year, with an option for a second year at the same rates And they want to start Monday."

He felt himself relax into a hazy reflection of Austin's elation.

Their path to this point wasn't like anything he'd imagined or planned for, when they first took their grandmother's inheritance and decided to build something that would give back to their community.

But it was starting to look like they might, at last, meet one of their major milestones. Mrs. Vallejo's commercial listing was about to go live. Nothing Abe had done—no funding tricks, or finagling of the books, or searches for an investor— had yet paid off. But here was Austin agitating his limbs like he was Kermit on show day, pulling a solution out of his goddamn joker's hat.

Like everything Abraham ever worked meticulously to build was a hilariously cute effort, and all they'd ever needed was for Awesome Austin to leap up into the sky and pull a raincloud full of gold down upon them.

The kid was grinning ear to ear. And even his grumpy ass wasn't surly enough to withhold the kudos his little brother deserved. "That's excellent, Austin. Forward us the contract; we'll add it to our loan application. I think FSCU is bound to approve us now. Hopefully in time for us to counter anyone who offers for this place."

"First right of refusal for the win." Austin snatched his cortado and finished it off. Like he needed more caffeine— Abe would need noise-canceling that night to drown out his brother's hours-long gaming session.

But he'd earned his giddiness. And Alicia would be stoked. She'd spent innumerable hours building the marketing side of their venture to keep them profitable. And Mateo had gotten himself onto the city council, partly to help them along with a growing list of local businesses with a Keep Surfside Swell initiative the two had dreamed up to keep chain competitors at bay.

So, yeah. He wasn't ranking high on anyone's perfection scale, but both his younger siblings were sailing easy, and helping them thrive had long been one of his primary goals. It was going to have to be enough to satisfy him.

Chapter Six

She was busy.

Once she'd acquired all her favorite supplies, she'd thrown herself into the work for the show. After all her pacing and thinking and arranging, the apartment was fine. Maybe not ideal, but fine. She had task lights, and she had the ocean to rest her eyes on when she needed to reset her perspective. She had printouts and enlargements from her photo archive, high-lighting details of the pieces she'd lost when her old apartment building burned. She had sketches, and studies, and a floor plan of The Wolfgang Lewis Gallery with notes about how to use the space to her best advantage.

In a way, it was a benefit. When Wolf first agreed to show her works, she'd gone back and forth with him about what he could use and how she could maximize what he was able to display. Now, she knew exactly how much would fit, and where, and how visitors would encounter the progression of her pieces as they moved through the space. She could get fucking precise with what potential buyers saw and felt.

Plus, she knew exactly which of her paintings Wolf had been convinced would sell well. She wasn't wasting time pouring her creative soul into anything she would then end up feeling negative about because the public wasn't clever enough to understand her brilliance.

So, yeah: she was busy. And her toil was paired with clarity, and purpose, and the kind of guaranteed success that not everyone got to embrace as they worked on artistic endeavors.

None of that should add up to her disconnected feeling as she worked on one of the mid-sized canvases she'd planned.

A rap on her door made her leap a bit, and turn down her music.

"Salt. You're here. Amazing. And Sofia." She smashed them both into a big hug. "Did I know you were coming over?"

Sofia smoothed back and tightened her ponytail. "No, we're a surprise."

Salt grinned. "If by surprise, you mean how you told us we should come by whenever."

She returned to her easel to clean up her brushes.

"Oh, don't stop working. I was actually hoping we could hang out while you painted for a bit. Like in the old days."

The smirk in Salt's voice lightened her heart. In college, their studio space was a frequent place for everyone to congregate and chat while several of them worked at their easels. She'd been forced to learn to enjoy working with people around during her socially isolated but constantly hemmed in years at the fine arts high school she'd attended. The joke/not a joke in college was that whatever time you showed up, Callie would be painting.

There was a lot of truth to it. But Callie wasn't the only one who put in a lot of hours. For all that he hadn't done much with his art since graduating, it seemed like Salt had shown up to his workspace almost every time Callie was there. And he wasn't the only one. But Sofia had claimed that Callie made her look good with all the other TAs, since none of their studios were as prone to buzz with activity. Even sometimes the buzz of students who weren't assigned to Callie's studio space, but showed up to grab any free easel or drafting table around her. Plus, there was that whole thing where Sofia had to move Callie's workstation from the corner, where she often ended up squeezed tight by other students, to a prime spot just opposite the door. It gave others room to hang out or work near her, and passers-by the chance to peek in and see if she was there before they popped into disturb anyone else who might be working.

So, okay, she'd been a rock star.

And fortunately for her and Wolfgang Lewis, she still was.

"So can we stay while you work, or will we be in your way?" Sofia asked, gauging her like she would intervene should Callie need her to.

But Salt was right. She'd never had a problem staying on task with people around. Plus, the work she'd produced in the studio Sofia supervised was fabulous enough to get her pieces on display outside of the college confines before she graduated. She'd even earned enough to fund a few guaranteed years of nothing but painting once she had her diploma.

Maybe her problem wasn't creating new work for Wolf— not that she'd quite gotten to the point of identifying her current situation as a problem. Maybe she'd focus and flow better if she allowed a busy creative environment to flourish around her.

"Did either of you bring anything to work on?"

Sofia's expression cleared as she tapped her large shoulder tote. "I have a few things I've been sketching out. I wouldn't mind curling up on your sofa while I do so."

Salt shrugged. "Nothing really for me. I can sit for you, if that would be helpful."

He knew all the ideas she'd been messing with for this series. He'd commented on one of her posts with a selection of her studies a few months back, and it had gotten them more in touch with each other than they'd been since college. He'd been her sounding board ever since.

She shrugged back at him. "Yeah, that can work. Let me reset what I'm doing."

"Sure, when you're ready. Do you two want any drinks? Snacks?" Salt asked.

Sofia lifted her hand. "See if Callie still has some of the apricot waters we brought over."

What she wanted was one of those cappuccinos from Pier Three, but it seemed rude to send Salt out for that when he'd just arrived. "Grab me one, too. Over ice if you don't mind."

He nodded. "On it."

After they started bustling, her work went okay. She put Salt in the same chair, at the same window, that Abraham had posed in. It was an entirely reasonable setup, and it had worked, annoyingly, ridiculously well for her first painting in Surfside. There was no special reason she could pinpoint why that earlier session felt more successful than the one with Salt.

When she'd painted Abraham, she hadn't yet spent any time doing all of the settling in and prep work that had occupied her whole week. And though she hadn't exactly asked Salt to come by and sit for her, he'd done so often enough in the past that working with him should have been familiar and easy.

They all three fell into a comfortable pattern of chat interspersed with focus. She'd hand it to them, it was as close to the vibe of her college studio as anywhere she'd worked in the years since. The fact that the vibe was no match for the for ... whatever it was that had her triple guessing her brushstrokes, wasn't on them.

Sofia, who seemed to have found her zone, startled when there was a knock at the door.

Between her palette, her pointed round brush, and her

short flat one, Callie was a bit stuck in place. "Come in," she called, because the last thing she needed was to dispatch Salt to the door when he'd finally settled into the angle she wanted from him.

She heard a slight grunt in the corridor before the doorknob turned and Abraham let himself in. He caught sight of the three of them. Sofia, back to lounging on the sofa, charcoal pencil in hand. Salt, not daring to glance away from the focus point that kept his chin aligned properly. Her.

By the time he finished sweeping the room with his gaze and let it rest on her, his eyes had done that deep and narrow thing that she hadn't captured quite right in her sketchpad.

"Stop right there," she said, swiveling to rest her brushes and snatch up the newsprint pad. "Just hold that thought for a minute."

Her hand flew over the page. She would have liked to keep going. To add the tension of his jaw, the tendons standing out on his neck. But she could get that later. The hard to capture, transient part was his eyes. And now she had them. Damn, she was good.

She dropped the pad triumphantly. "Hey, Abraham. Thanks. What's up?"

"You just let anyone come in without checking who it is first?"

She batted at the air to dismiss his concern. "Hands were full."

His own hand was wedging a coffee cup out of the crook of his left elbow.

"Is that for me?"

His expression disdained her for making assumptions, but he handed it over. "It's one of those cappuccinos you like. Alicia asked me to drop it to you on my way home."

She clapped a couple of times. "Fantastic. I love that woman. She knows how to feed an addiction. Gimme."

She was already taking it from him when she made her demand, sipping it before she remembered to thank him for delivering it. She must have made a face.

"Did it get too cold?"

"No?" She sipped again. "Temp is fine. It's just not quite like the one you made before."

"But it's still fine?"

"It's good. Thank you. Nice of you to make it."

"I'm not the one who made it." He took a step backward. Some trickster was plucking at her sternum, encouraging her to shrink the space between them again. But she wasn't following the lead of any impish spirits.

"Well, send me your schedule so I know when you're working. Then I can swing by and get your special version whenever I'd like." She tried the cappuccino again. It wasn't bad, not at all—just not, somehow, as good as the other one. Too much vanilla maybe.

Abraham was studying how Salt was studying the barometer mounted to the balcony wall. "Just go any time. Anyone can replicate it. There's nothing I can do for you that's singular in any way."

Callie looked between the two men in her apartment. Was Abraham annoyed she had another sitter? Welcome to her life. You didn't get to be as renowned for semi-magical figurative work as she was without roping lots of people into being artist models. She turned back to taunt him for his temper, but he was already walking away.

Chapter Seven

Bonfire nights had been his idea.

The beaches north of Pier Three—the surfing side, in other words, as opposed to the fishing side—featured a number of fire rings dotted along them. They went first come first serve to beach-goers, and since he or his siblings were pretty much always at Pier Three Coffee at closing time, it seemed obvious that they could keep an eye on the fire rings and hop out to snag a free one as it was getting on towards sunset.

The bonfire nights started out as just them and their cousin Noah, who ran a local surf shop. And also Noah's friend Mateo, back when he was just the source of their baked goods, and not his sister's paramour. Sometimes a couple other early to bed / early to rise people they knew. And it grew from there.

Over the years, they got to be such regulars that the other locals took their use of the fire ring closest to the cafe as a given. The expanding circle of friends drifted there on Friday nights year-round, drinking and watching the sun set over the

Pacific. A respite full of reconnection and releasing the stresses of the previous week.

His backpack for bonfires was bright orange, and insulated, and could hold a dozen beers. Other stuff, too: a bottle opener, bags to collect the recycling and beach trash, bug repellent, a pair of flip flops and a quick-dry towel in case he decided to head into the water. But he'd splurged on the orange one for the robust insulation. He liked his beer cold and plentiful.

He didn't typically go through both six packs on his own. The point of bonfire nights was to connect with friends, to share, but he stayed off the Saturday shift schedule so he could indulge if he wanted.

He was popping open a can when his cousin loomed over him, blocking out the view of the setting sun. "You started without me?"

He handed Noah the beer and grabbed another for himself. Noah took it upon himself to relocate the backpack so he could occupy the sand beside him. "What's the occasion?"

"No occasion." He drank deeply.

Noah grunted. It was a grunt that said, "I'm three weeks older than you and I know when you're making stuff up."

Abraham grunted right back, because three weeks wasn't all that much, not over the course of a few decades. So Noah could just stifle that fake superiority of his. After finishing the beer, he asked about a music festival up in the city his cousin had attended.

Noah fell for his diversion, pulling out his portable speaker to cue up some new band he was excited about.

Three weeks younger or not, Abraham had the skills to manage the kid, just like he did for his sister and brother. For all the siblings and cousins who grew up together in Surfside.

Or so he thought, right up until Noah nudged him. "So, baby brother saved the day, huh?"

"You'll find that the three of us worked collectively towards this goal," he replied, which ... yeah. Totally skipped over about four hundred of the feelings rumbling around his chest cavity ever since Austin signed the contract with the fishing collective. But those little darts of jealousy, obsolescence, frustration, pride, and anger could just piss right off.

Well, not the pride. He held on to the pride. He wasn't an entire jerk, just someone who found himself no longer so useful to his family.

"Sure, you're all three heroic and amazing. But Austin's the one whose plan actually worked, right?"

Abraham decided to continue the trend of uselessness by failing to snag another beer for his cousin. "How about you let it go now?"

"Mmm. Sure." Noah sounded casual, but he knew better than to trust his gleaming eyes. Sure enough, Noah let out one of his piercing whistles—Abe presumed it was a side tease about how he couldn't whistle—and called across the fire pit. "Hey, Sally."

The university librarian looked up, all attentive. So did pretty much the entire rest of the circle. "Hey, Noah."

"Did you hear that Abraham here has become an artist's model? Picture it. All these fine muscles and chiseled lines immortalized in acrylics."

"Oils," he corrected, and bit back his other comments.

Just one word was enough to egg on his cousin. "Oils. I sit corrected. That's classy, dude. Though I worry you're going to get to be too fancy now to park yourself in the sand and drink beer with us. Gonna be so busy living the glamorous life you can't hang out anymore. Parties, raves, gallery openings."

"What do you think he does now?" Austin asked. "Sometimes I can barely sleep from all the disco lights and techno beats coming from our apartment."

His brother fell back laughing when Abraham gestured at him with his left arm. It was a move he came up with back in middle school, to flip off Austin with plausible deniability. After all, there were no fingers in play. He'd very cleverly—to his young mind—kept the deniability in place by sometimes letting himself be caught flipping off his brother with his right hand. It was just enough cover to allow him all the vestigial-limb flipping off that his younger brother so often deserved.

"So it's true, then, that Callie Hamasaki is your new neighbor?" Sally asked.

Austin sat up. "Yeah, why? Do you know her?"

Sally shook her head. "I wish. I've been working at the library for nine years now, and I must have read at least three or four big profiles of her in the alumni magazine in that time. At least one of them was before she even graduated."

Austin took over the gossip rounds, collecting everyone's attention in that effortless way of his as he told them about the fire, and Callie having lost so much work. Sally was passing her phone around, showing some of the press about Callie's skyrocket of a career and the praise that seemed to come from all over the world for her. Austin launched into some tale about the way a couple of his college friends got beyond excited once when Austin spotted one of her exhibition posters on campus and mentioned that his sister roomed with the art phenom.

While his brother held everyone rapt, Abraham shifted his orange backpack closer and grabbed another beer.

She paced around the living room—heel toe, heel toe, heel toe —hoping desperately that if she spent another ten or thirty minutes thinking about it, the solution to the nonsense of her Salt canvas would come to her.

She'd done all the things already. Everything she'd ever learned or stumbled across, in over two decades of painting, that set her on the right path when she was feeling a bit lost. She'd done her favorite yoga and meditation routine. She'd slept on it. She'd worked on something else.

That at least had gone well.

She'd switched from the canvas back to her sketchbook, constructing elaborate studies and variations. She'd gone for a long walk by the shore. She'd screamed into her pillow. She'd dug a brand new journal out of the mishmash of things her friends had deposited in a crate by her sofa, and worked on her artist statement for the gallery show, articulating how this piece fit into it.

She'd practically set up an altar to the gods of creativity, pleading for guidance.

Finally, she'd called Sofia over, and was now leaning right into the drama of it all by waving her arms around as she explained all the supposedly surefire steps that had failed to help.

At last she stopped in front of her friend and planted her hands on her hips. "So, what is it? What's wrong with this piece, and what do I do about it?"

Sofia reached out and tugged Callie to sit beside her. "What if there's no answer to your question?"

She slumped. Suddenly she remembered all too well this feeling of wanting her mentor to flick her magic fingers and show her how to fix things, only to have her stubbornly stick to the premise that Callie was going to have to fix it herself. Including finding the solution on her own.

"I'm a sounding board, not a project manager," Sofia used to say, which could not have been less useful.

Now she patted at Callie's knee like it was a true consolation. "If you can't tell what's wrong, it could be that there's nothing wrong."

That jerked her forward from the naval, to flail anew. "Obviously there's something wrong. Look at it."

Sofia did so, lips pursed. Agonizing minutes later, she looked back at Callie. "What?"

"What do you mean, 'what?'" She was basically begging now, but screw it. She needed Sofia's help.

"What's wrong with it? Explain it to me."

"If I knew what was wrong, I would know how to fix it."

Sofia didn't drop her calm demeanor. "Would you?"

"Well, I mean, probably. I'd be a lot further along anyway."

"So, there's something wrong, and you can't describe it, but you know it's true."

"Right."

"And no matter how much you bash your head against it, you can't figure it out?"

"I'm not—okay, maybe I am bashing my head, but I didn't start by bashing my head."

"How did you start?"

Something in her voice alerted Callie that Sofia had trapped her, but Callie was too desperate to be wary. "You saw me. It was when you and Salt came over that first time. He sat down, I started painting. Simple as that."

"And what were you doing before we came over?"

Callie gestured at a canvas leaning against the kitchen wall. "Finishing that one."

Sofia nodded. "And we interrupted you."

"Yeah, but that's fine. I got back to it and finished it later. And there's nothing wrong with it. Obviously. Look at it." She sounded like a petulant braggart.

Sofia's glance over her glasses made it clear that she wasn't alone in thinking so.

"Sorry. Yeah. Anyway, I finished it, and it's what I was looking for. I'm happy with it. And it didn't make any difference that you guys came over, because I enjoyed working on it while I was on my own, and I enjoyed having you guys around while I was painting Salt. The timing of it all is not the problem."

Sofia's nod was slow and not serene. "I remember you had all these plans and studies tacked up when we got here. Do you want to tell me the story about them?"

"I mean, it's not much of a story. It's just what I laid out to create for The Wolfgang Lewis Gallery show."

"You made a deliberate plan for that?"

"Sure, of course. I've got to be efficient. I know what Wolf likes, and what works well in his space. And also what I'm exploring with my work. It's all pretty simple. Or, straightforward, anyway, if not simple."

"Okay. And then we got here, and you started to work on Salt. Is the painting of him one that you had figured out in your initial scheme?"

"Well, no. I wasn't going to do this one, but it works. It's just a little bit of a change from what I planned. But that doesn't ..." She trailed off.

"It doesn't what?" Sofia asked.

Callie sighed. "It doesn't mean I can't bash my head against the wall until I make it work. Except, obviously, it does. I'm trying to force it and mistaking the ability to work quickly with the ability to bypass the thinking process before I begin that quick work."

Her friend laughed and pulled her in for a hug. "Okay. I guess you know what to do."

The hell of it was, she did.

Chapter Eight

He'd curse himself for a fool, but it seemed ridiculous to add such tired complaints to the too-stuffed sack of negative self-talk he kept forcibly emptying.

Besides which, his sister and brother were entirely smug, with their raised eyebrows and little hums at each other, when he mixed up an oat milk cappuccino just before his shift ended. But if Alicia didn't want him making her friend a drink, she shouldn't have gone out of her way to tease him about Callie complaining that his concoction was better than hers.

Alicia could stand to spend a little less time conveying things about him to others. Since she wasn't, he was behaving the way she so clearly wanted him to, and he wasn't going to stand around waiting for his siblings to pass judgment.

Her door was open, the corridor swelling with a burst of what, last time, he'd confirmed, was K-pop. At least he didn't have to juggle the drink to knock this time. If he was going to keep doing this—not that he had any intention of continuously carting drinks to her door—he should grab a couple of his reusable thermoses so he could stash her coffee in the side pocket of his work backpack.

But since he wasn't making a habit of bringing her cappuccinos, it didn't really matter.

The whole circus of her friends was spread across the apartment, including a couple dancing on the balcony, and three people in some sort of tickling/wrestling match on the sofa. The guy who'd been posing shirtless last time leaned against the kitchen wall, flipping through a sketchbook of what were clearly more of Callie's drawings. One of the crate-carrying guys from move-in day hovered over her shoulder, watching her draw. Somehow, even though she was sitting quiet and alone at the two person dining table, Callie was the center of it all.

No one paid him any attention as he came in. So he decided to ignore them in return, sitting down opposite her.

"Oat milk cappuccino." He slid it to within her grabbing distance.

She had it halfway to her mouth before she glanced up. "Oh, hey. Is it vanilla?"

He nodded. Of course it was. He'd already put up with an earful from Alicia, asking why exactly his version of the drink was superior to hers. He didn't have an answer, so he'd ignored her questions. But he'd caught her narrowed-eyed attention, trying to spy on his every move when he'd concocted it earlier.

"Where's mine?" the crate guy asked. He leaned over like he would help himself to a sip before Callie even tasted it.

"Back off, Curtis," she said, prompting a laugh from some of the people on the sofa.

He wasn't sure, not having paid that much attention to them when they first came around, but he thought at least a couple of the people there were new to this whole cavorting cadre of hers.

Callie set the coffee just beyond the edge of her sketchbook and resumed her work. "It's great, thanks."

He nodded again, not that she was looking, and settled in to watch her for a bit. She was bobbing her head to the music and swaying a little, but nothing disrupted the flow of her hand over the paper.

He wasn't at all familiar with her job. Hadn't even watched Bob Ross painting landscapes while battling insomnia, like his college roommate Ernesto used to. But it seemed like she possessed limitless amounts of focus and confidence as she worked. Maybe he would search out those articles about her that Sally had mentioned.

Hell, if he was going to be featured in one of her pieces, maybe he should invest some serious time in figuring out more about what made her, in particular, such a shining star.

The couple who'd been on the patio came in. When they clocked that the one who had been her model was looking through drawings, they bounded over and crowded in to see. One of them shoved Abraham's chair while he was at it, jolting him against the table.

"Hey," Callie said, lifting her head to glare at him.

He opened his mouth to apologize about her marred drawing and nearly spilled oat milk, but the newcomer jumped in.

"Oh my god, Callie, that was so my fault. I'm so sorry. I was hyper focused on checking out what Salt was viewing, and didn't even notice that I would be pushing this guy around. Guy, listen ..." He must have clocked Abraham's missing limb, because his face went through a familiar set of contortions while he pieced together some words. "Damn, guy, I am such a debacle. Did I smash your wound site? Do you need, like, a bandage or something?"

"Jesus Christ, Liam," snapped the model guy, who apparently was named Salt. The scorn in Salt's tone snapped Abe's brain out of its circling blankness.

He held up his arm. "Do I look like I've got an oozing sore? Or maybe you think you knocked into me so hard my hand just fell off right here at the table?"

"Seriously, Liam?" Callie set a blotting sheet over her page, and closed the newsprint pad.

Liam's face looked frozen in anguish as he half-crouched over Abraham.

"Why are you saying rude and ridiculous things in my house? I mean, I love all you people, and you've all been great at helping me get set up here, but I know for damn sure that Sofia told you my open hours were for people who were going to do some work while you're here, not dancing, or insulting people, or," she gestured back at the sofa, "making cuddle piles."

She heard shuffling behind her that she assumed was Amity and them straightening themselves up a bit. Not that she really minded when they brought their happy love vibes to her place. It was peaceful in its way. And she'd been totally in the flow until Abraham showed up with his ridiculously delicious cappuccino and sat across from her.

Liam stepped back and dropped his head. "I'm sorry for acting the fool, guy. Shit. And Callie, I apologize. I was so super stoked to see your sketches. You know how inspiring you are, and here I go blundering around messing up your work and disturbing you and blurting out rudeness. I offer my sincerest."

He reached towards Abraham for a handshake, then glanced real quick at the man's arm. Making sure, she was guessing, that he wasn't turning the interaction more awkward. "Liam Cooke."

Abraham grunted as he shook his hand, and waited about two beats longer than was polite before offering up his own name.

Liam took another step back. "Hey. So. Are you an artist, too?"

Abraham stood and shouldered his backpack. "Nope." He glanced quickly around the room, then turned his attention back to Callie. "Enjoy your happy hour."

And then he just left. Walked off without giving her a chance to correct him. Not that she needed to bother. She bet he knew perfectly well that he'd gotten it wrong. Bet he'd done it deliberately.

Jerk.

Liam inched back towards her, but Salt took the chair before he could, stacking her first sketchpad atop the one in front of her. "Am I getting a kind of, like, mythic vibe off these? Not high fantasy or anything. I just mean ... maybe a timelessness to the way you investigate form."

"I was gonna say that," Liam claimed. "There's definitely a timeless feel to these, like your distilling the history of art or something."

"No, not that," Salt said, and she might have grinned at him if he weren't being such an earnest crusader for her. "It's not a distillation. You're not taking from anything. It's like you ..."

He studied the finished pieces she'd propped against the wall beside him.

"They're sculptural," Amity said.

"Yeah, that, too. The way you mix softer lines with the hyperreal wings pulls our focus in a new way. We can't apply our usual understanding to them—we have to think differently."

"So innovative," Liam blurted.

She rolled her eyes. He wasn't terrible. But damn was she annoyed at him for being so careless with Abraham, both in his actions and in his words.

Alicia was her best friend.

She didn't need any awkwardness coming her way because some guy she hung out with way back in undergrad was boorish with her brother.

Chapter Nine

He was wearing a suit and tie, so what did she think was happening when she opened her door as he passed?

He probably wouldn't have paused for her comment, but once again she was letting in a half dozen members of her entourage.

It wasn't his business. He should be able to admit that. But how many times was she going to just invite in these random artsy types while she was supposedly hard at work on her various masterpieces? If she was as busy as Alicia claimed, how did she manage all of these interlopers, wandering in and out at all hours?

"You off to get the coffee on?" she asked him, so smiling and cocksure as he sidestepped the person arriving with an easel and backpack. At least that one seemed intent on doing something artistic, as opposed to goofing around like the thoughtless jerk who'd bashed into him.

It was possible he was in a mood and overstating the problem.

"No, I don't pour drinks in my best suit," he said. "If you

want a cappuccino, you'll have to send one of your minions for it."

One of the minions laughed, but Abraham had places to go. He didn't hang around to find out how Callie silenced her.

Yes, he could have been more neighborly, but, eh. His parents weren't around to scold him, and his brother was meeting him at the title company. Austin hadn't bothered to come home and change after his shift. He'd intimated that Abraham was going overboard by pulling his suit out of the dry cleaning bag. But all he had to do was imagine the look on the face of his thesis advisor if he dared to show up looking less than professional for something as momentous as their closing on Pier Three.

He was not that guy. Let Austin laugh, if it suited him. But Abraham was suiting up.

Alicia was dressed up, too, though she indulged in her usual litany of complaints about her corporate wardrobe. He gave her a big hug, so she knew he appreciated it. And then he gave Austin a big hug because the kid didn't deserve side eye from him, having been basically the one to save their entire asses with his brainstorms.

Abraham wasn't any more sanguine than before about how that meant he'd failed his siblings. But his brother deserved his due.

Signing the paperwork didn't actually take that much of their time. Nothing compared to the hours they'd put into getting the loan approved in the first place, and making the official offer to Mrs. Vallejo. He kind of felt like it should've been harder on them. Something more than just strolling into the title company and signing a few dozen times.

Even pausing to read over all the documents, checking they were in accord with what they'd previewed, didn't draw the process out very much. He didn't have time to get overheated in his suit, much less for his prosthetic socket to pinch, before they were back on the street.

The Wells siblings were the official owners of the building that housed Pier Three Coffee, give or take their credit union's lien, and the years' worth of financial reports he would be running to support their loan.

They stood looking at each other. His siblings' eyes were twinkling. Probably his were, too. And it didn't matter how they'd gotten there.

His entire self relaxed into the sensation. "We did it."

Alicia squeaked out a laugh that set them all off. "I'm so damn happy."

"I don't think it's hit me yet," Austin said. "But, yeah, happy."

"Same," he said, and neither of them acted surprised, or put out, when he wrapped them into another hug.

"So we're going out to celebrate?" Austin asked.

He checked the time. "Too early for beers?"

Alicia laughed. "Well, I'm certainly not going to suggest we go for coffee. I'll hold off on that until we're at our place."

"Our place." Austin grinned, looking up from his navigation app. "There's a joint a few blocks away I've been meaning to check out, if you're game."

Alicia gestured to the door. "Lead on, little brother."

An hour or so later, Abraham made a pretense of offering his siblings the last of the pitcher.

Alicia shook her head. "Callie and I are going out to dinner tonight. I should stop now or I'll need a power nap before I'm good for anything."

"So at bonfire," he started.

His brother interrupted to ask Alicia, "Where were you guys anyway?"

"It was Greg and Marie's anniversary dinner," Alicia said. "I know we texted you about it."

Austin shrugged. "Must have missed it."

"That's code for he muted our group text again," Abraham said.

"What's code for someone doesn't want to admit we're right about his obsession with Leyla?" she responded.

Austin reached over like he would swipe the last of the beer right out of Abraham's hand. He wasn't about to let that happen. "Point is, Sally was talking about all these times the alumni magazine had articles about Callie. And when I was dropping off that drink for her, it seemed like ... I mean, whatever, but is she really such a big deal? Like, beyond the Bay Area?"

Austin snorted. "How are you ignorant of this? She's some kind of powerhouse. I don't know about her first couple of years, but by the time I was on campus, you couldn't cross the quad without running into some poster bragging on her. I was out with this art major once and mentioned that Alicia was her roommate and the woman went nearly stalker on me, trying to persuade me to engineer a meeting. Something about an installation in New York that happened right after you two graduated."

"Now that was intense," Alicia said. "They sent an actual stylist to our hotel room to get Callie ready for the opening. We still talk about the charcuterie plate they sent up that afternoon. It was beyond."

He nodded. Okay. He was beginning to understand what a big deal Callie was, but still. "Does that kind of constant adulation thing happen a lot with her? Cause it seems like every time I see her, there's a ..." He stopped, because saying 'a hovering crowd of sycophants' sounded like something his siblings would quote back to him on repeat for decades.

Alicia nodded. "It's not like we can't go out in public without her being mobbed or anything. She's not an A-list celebrity. But, yeah, she's got a lot of admirers, given that her career is still young. I think *Modern Perspective* is going to mention the fire in their next issue. Though maybe that's part of Wolfgang Lewis promoting his show."

So it seemed Callie was as magnificent as she said she was. Good for her owning that level of self confidence and personal power. He knew plenty of people—himself included—could stand to have a higher natural regard for themselves. To move through the world like they believed in themselves. Hadn't Abraham just spent too many days in a row wondering if he'd outlived his usefulness to his siblings? Buying the building was the last real growth goal he'd set for his side of the business. With it, now Alicia and Austin could build Pier Three's success with the help of any random accountant, instead of him specifically.

He quashed the self-pity, because it sat way too close to the thought patterns that led to internalized ableism, and his brain didn't need to host that shit. The reality was, his siblings kept showing their mettle as they built Pier Three together. Between Austin's brainstorms and labor to convert the conference suite, and Alicia's marketing plan that established them as part of a newly visible consortium of local businesses, they had pulled their cafe out of danger, and given them the chance to meet larger goals like this purchase. Everything Abraham contributed came from what they'd all set in place years ago, when they first opened the coffee shop and signed their partnership agreement.

It left him wondering what, exactly, his brother, his sister, or their business needed from him, specifically, uniquely, in order to thrive.

And why, exactly, he came up empty when he tried to name what he could do for himself to specifically and uniquely thrive, too.

He drained the beer and made a mental note to cultivate some new personal and professional goals, along with more self-regard.

Chapter Ten

It was pure nerves and nonsense, the way she was shoving furniture around to create a viewing space for her work.

Wolf, on his way to a wedding down south, had arranged to swing by Surfside in transit. He wanted to take a look at what she'd been working on. Nothing unusual or difficult about that, given her unusually difficult circumstances of the fire destroying a chunk of what he'd been planning to show. It was even an advantage, she reminded herself, to get his reaction at the stage. She still had time to pivot, if necessary.

Not that it would be necessary, since her work was genius, as always. And Wolf was discerning enough to see it at this stage, in these suboptimal conditions, and still recognize the treasure she was laying at his feet.

She heard something in the hall and bopped over to turn off her Bluetooth speaker.

"... constant foot traffic around here," somebody was saying.

Abraham, that's who it was. She wasn't sure when she'd gotten to the point of differentiating his cadence from his brother's, but it hardly mattered. What mattered was what he was saying.

"This huge crowd of people constantly traipsing in and out. If I wanted to spend my day directing traffic, I'd have become a librarian."

"A librarian?" That was Wolf, and Callie did not like the pitch of his voice. She'd heard that tone before, and recognized the offense in it.

She lurched forward, eager to interrupt before Abraham could finish whatever anecdote he was relaying about some library down the street.

She threw the door wide. "Wolf! You made it, great."

"Callie, my wunderkind." He moved in for a hug.

They exchanged double cheek kisses, and she was turning to shut the door when she noticed Abraham was still standing there. She cocked her head at him. "Help you?"

He shrugged off his backpack and reached for a Pier Three-branded insulated cup in the side pocket. "Your usual," he said, holding it out.

"Was I expecting you?"

"Seems like you expect people twenty-four/seven around here. Are they ever going to remember your apartment number, or should I just expect to direct everyone I meet in the foyer to you?"

"I don't remember asking for you to be my concierge," she snapped. And maybe she'd have maintained the whole of the high ground, if she hadn't snagged the drink from him before closing the door in his face.

Damn his barista skills anyway.

She turned to Wolf. "Well, in addition to bubbly water and tea, now I can offer you a cappuccino."

"Friend of yours?"

She shook her head. "My best friend's brother. One of them anyway. They own a coffee shop, and their parents own this apartment building. He sometimes drops off a cappuccino on his way home from work."

"Service with a smile. I see."

Good thing she hadn't been sipping the drink, or she'd have snarfed it up her nose. "It is not his trademark. Anyway, sorry if he was going after you. I don't entirely get why he needs to be so grumpy about my guests."

"He was a tad uncivilized," Wolf said, and Callie tried to hide her wince.

It wasn't that Wolfgang Lewis was bound to hold Abraham's rudeness against her, but the man was definitely used to dealing with people who valued both his opinions and his presence.

She didn't intend to coddle him, but she also didn't need her beautiful new paintings fighting an uphill battle to be appreciated by the man whose partnership would make her thousands of dollars.

"If only everyone could be tamed by the beauty of the world," she said lightly, abandoning the drink in her kitchen and leading him further into the room. "And speaking of beauty ..."

She spread her arms wide, gesturing to the canvases she'd displayed for his attention. "Welcome to my temporary studio."

He pursed his lips. "Ah, Callie. I still can't comprehend the enormity of our loss. That Jesse Mockrin-inspired triptych of the parasailing dragonflies. I had the perfect buyer for it, and now ..." He shook his head.

Callie agreed. Of course she did. She'd been the one who'd spent hours creating the luminous iridescence of the wings. Not to mention that working on that trio had brought her to the point where she felt she'd truly cracked the code to exploring the androgynous and the feminine sensuality of the male form. There was no question that the fire had been a massive setback.

Yes, she reminded herself constantly of the advantage she'd had coming out of it. Not just in a 'nobody was hurt and it's all just possessions' sort of way. But because she'd been able to find her footing so quickly in Alicia's apartment, and had her contract with Wolf to spur her into immediate creation. And she'd been surrounded with the support of her community. But when she gave herself time to think about it, she wanted to spiral into a ball and build a protective shell around herself so she didn't have to face processing the actual loss.

She'd survived upheavals in the past, and come out better on the other side. Eventually. There was absolutely no reason to believe it would be any different this time.

"Well," Wolf said, approaching the first of the canvases.

"Well, indeed."

"Let's see what you've got." They'd done this before: his silent inspections while she sat back and attempted to view her work through the eyes of someone new.

Part of the reason—a huge part—The Wolfgang Lewis Gallery was such a success was Wolf's discernment and ability to recognize what would sell. What would bring in major buzz. What would excite the art world.

He wasn't known for discovering new talent. But he was renowned for elevating artists from mid-range success to national, or even international, recognition. Which was, of course, precisely what her career needed. She'd made a living via her painting since she was in college. But now she was on the verge of leveling up.

And she wanted it.

Desperately.

It was everything she'd been working towards.

He circled back around at last, having expressed little more than a few hums and one stroke of his chin as he surveyed everything. No one would call her thin-skinned, but this was her first time displaying everything new at once. She wouldn't have objected to some gushing on Wolf's part.

"Yes, well." He met her eye for perhaps not quite long enough before turning back to her work. "I see where you're going with this. The kind of light/dark butterfly thing here in particular."

He paused in front of the canvas based on Abraham.

"*Moth-erflying*," she said, though she wasn't yet tied to the name. The dark side of the torso sprouted a wing based on the Red Lacewing butterfly. The wing on the bright side was very similar to that of a Peppered Moth. Both wings curved forward, as if to cradle the torso, rather than arching back for flight like those on the painting based on Salt.

She quite liked the way the Abraham painting suggested comfort and protection, even as his wings shot teasing shadows over the distinctly masculine lines of his torso and face. She breathed easier that Wolfgang got it.

And then he turned to the table with the small canvases.

Whoever trained Wolfgang in the art of the compliment sandwich forgot to let him know about body language. She caught herself mirroring his slight recoil, which just prompted her to bite her lips as she straightened up. But really, this was the whole point of his visit: to let her know where she was fucking up so she could course-correct.

"I don't understand why your colors are coming off so muddy on all these. Instead of being in conversation with Mockrin, like the dragonflies were, these set out to hurl compost at those rich, lush, classic colors." He carried a couple of the foot-square canvases to the window. "It's not down to the light in here, no. I will say the compositions are beautiful. And I'm entranced by your heavy brushstrokes on the small scale works. But the eye, Callie. It just wants to bounce off of these in search of something else. And that is distinctly not what I think you're going for. At least, it's not anything I've seen from you before, and I'd be surprised to hear that you were aiming for that with these."

"Mmm," she said, which wasn't much of a defense of her efforts.

"I don't mean to discourage you, my dear. I don't entirely fear you won't get the show rebuilt on time. Especially if we can see more of your moths and butterflies, and maybe you can ruminate on those poor lost dragonflies. I'm sure you can manage."

She just blinked at him.

"Are you devastated? I don't want to rush off to my event when you're in a spiral."

Callie shook her head. "No, it's fine. I'm fine."

He squeezed her shoulders. "Listen. Enjoy that coffee from the rude friend. Take a walk on the beach or something. And then come back to your easel and attack the canvas with new fervor."

"Right. I will. It'll be fine. Of course."

"Good," he nodded and checked his watch. "I'm off. I'll check in ... what, three weeks? And as long as everything shapes up by then, I don't have to worry about finding someone new for those dates."

Chapter Eleven

Heading out for his next shift, he nearly tripped over the thermos he'd left with Callie. She must have deposited it on their doorstep sometime between the late hour when Austin got home from his date, and the early one when Abraham left for work.

Her door was shut; all was silent. He didn't think about her much at all as he went through his day.

Processing the quarterly bonus checks ended up taking longer than he'd expected, so he decided he may as well grab a macchiato and a couple of that morning's pastries to take home. And since he had her cleaned out thermos with him, also a vanilla oat milk cappuccino for Callie. Neither of his siblings were on shift just then, which spared him the taunts.

Callie welcomed him. Told him to come on in. He was, for no good reason, too tongue tied to explain that he was just dropping off the drink. He ended up on her sofa, passing over the pastry bag so she could take her pick.

"You're wearing your arm today."

Shaking his own drink to disperse the flavors now that the ice had melted a bit, he thought back. Other than when he'd been in his suit on the way to the closing, he hadn't been around her much with his prosthesis on. "I don't don it much during summer, unless I'll be on the computer a bunch."

He held it out for examination, because everyone always wanted to examine it.

Instead of grabbing, she drew a finger along the carbon fiber exterior. It should not have generated goosebumps on his sound arm, but maybe his hand was cold from the drink.

"It doesn't get in the way when you're serving customers?"

He reached for the almond croissant she hadn't chosen. "No. This terminal device—the hand—is largely waterproof. It's the only good option for my work environment, as long as I protect the wrist socket. I can even back-flush the espresso machine. But I pull drinks and everything just as well without it, unless I'm trying to make latte art, when I need it to keep the cup at the correct angle. But no matter what, I'm not much good at art."

"I was just thinking that I would need a prosthetic to hold my palate when painting en plein air. Hell, I haven't thought about what parts of my job it'd be vital for me to have a left hand. Hefting and stretching canvases, probably. It's not like I don't use my left hand plenty, to squeeze out pigments." She began to mime what he presumed were everyday actions for her. "Hold the wipe rag. Steady myself while I'm doing fine work. But I'm sure I could find a workaround for all those things. I'm just used to having both hands, so that's what I use."

"Whereas I've never had a left hand. I've always been able to get on without it. At least for most things."

She dropped her gaze to his crotch and then back up, smirking. And there went the goose bumps again.

"Ha. Very droll," he said.

"You were the one talking about making foam art."

He groaned at her abominable joke, hoping his banter

didn't sound like he was half strangled by the bolt of the lust she'd inspired. He aimed to distract them both by showing off how the myoelectric controls allowed him to switch between the finger grip settings he'd programmed, and finished up with the best party trick, the three-sixty rotation from the wrist. People always loved that one.

Callie grinned, curling her legs up onto the sofa. "Glad you brought the drink, by the way. I need the kick, so I can stay up working tonight."

Abraham winced. "Yeah, so, it's an apology cappuccino."

"And muffin."

"And muffin, yes. I was not especially generous when your broker came by the other day."

"Owner of the gallery for my upcoming show. But, yeah, we noticed."

He scrubbed his hand through his hair. "Shit."

"Yeah, I wouldn't have minded him being in a better mood the first time he saw all my replacement pieces." She nudged him with her foot. "He did really like the one of you."

He could feel the heat of his cheeks. "He did? Okay, that's good then. Can I see it? Is that okay to ask?"

Looking at him, practically holding his breath waiting for her answer, she absolutely had to fuck with him.

"I mean, it's a little salacious but ..."

"Salacious?"

"Don't worry, nothing overt. Your mom and your sister didn't seem to mind too much about the nudity."

He coughed. "My mom and sister?"

"Yep." She nodded with tons of enthusiasm. "I told Alicia about it over dinner the other night. When she was dropping me off after, she asked if she could come in and see. She thought to invite your folks down to check it out while we were at it."

Abraham wedged his drink between those long thighs of his, and crumpled up the pastry bag, concentrating on it like he wasn't trying to hide red cheeks. "Both my parents?"

"Well, no, your dad was out with friends that night. So it was just your mom." She sipped the cappuccino. "Don't worry. Like I said, it isn't very salacious. Even when your dad does see it, I don't think he'll be too discombobulated."

The other fun part about teasing him was how it served to lower his expectations. When she had models who were used to the art scene, she always ended up with glowing feedback, but to people who weren't used to the experience, she never knew what kind of baseline they'd bring to viewing her stuff. Jokes about latte art aside, Abraham never struck her as much of an aficionado. He definitely seemed to have basic questions about what was happening every time he stopped by.

"Maybe I'll ..." His jaw shifted. "No, you know what? Alicia has seen it. It's better that I do, too."

She hopped up to pull out the canvas, because any more watching him writhe in discomfort would set her into a fit of giggles. And that would give the game away, and maybe risk his never coming back so she could fuck with him some more.

She rested it, back side to him, on the coffee table. "Ready?"

He squinched those deep brown eyes of his, like he was braced to squeeze them shut, or struggling to open them properly. He drew in a breath. "Ready."

She flipped it around fast, because drawing out the reveal would absolutely make her collapse. She wished she'd managed to record this whole interaction to show Alicia later. Her friend always called her older brother the grim one, and she knew Alicia would revel in all of the details. Somehow, though, Callie wasn't sure if she could do justice to the way everything in Abraham seemed to release at once when he saw the painting.

His posture relaxed. He blew out his breath. And his eyes —they went so soft, and just a bit wide. It must have been the refraction of light off her canvas that made them seem to glow.

"That's. Wow, Callie. You—" He pressed his lips together, shook his head again. "Wow."

She bowed her chin in acknowledgement of his praise.

Then he shot her a mock glare. "Nice winding me up there."

Her chest fizzed with the pleased giggle she was not releasing. "Your mom cried."

"Of course she did. She still has our construction paper turkey handprints from elementary school. Pulls them out to decorate the sideboard every Thanksgiving."

"That is so sweet. Wait, did yours trace your right hand?"

His grin was quicksilver and sparked something dangerous against those fluttering giggles she hadn't yet released.

"I wasn't gonna let somebody else trace my hand for me. And I didn't have the dexterity to do it with my left. So I traced my prosthetic. It's the least turkey-like turkey ever created."

She tilted her head. "Yes, I'm remembering this now. Does it have a bunch of orange and green feathers glued to it?"

"Isn't it beautiful?" This grin was softer and more amused than any of his she'd yet seen. She was not investigating the fact that she could catalog all of his rare grins now.

"I sincerely thought that was supposed to be some kind of tree to go with the turkeys. Damn, I wish I'd asked at the time. That is hilarious."

"Right? So, yeah. I'm not surprised she cried." He cleared his throat. "I might, too. It's amazing Callie. I'm honored."

Chapter Twelve

That was nice: he wasn't complaining or rude. Abraham may be no connoisseur, but she was prepared to accept his astounded adulation.

He leaned forward until he was almost face to face with his image, studying it close like it was a mirror, and not her interpretation of his form through the lens of her artistic sensibility.

"You made me look kind of beautiful," he said, with a wrinkle in his brow.

She didn't know if he was mystified, or what. She leaned the canvas back a bit to look at it from above. Damn, but she was great with color and light. Even upside down the flow was strong.

"I was in this history of art class once. And the professor was explaining that shunga—erotic art dating back to the Heian period, though it got really popular with woodblock prints in the Edo period—are called that because shunga is Japanese for spring. He made some throwaway comment about artists needing to capture the fleeting nature of female beauty. He should draw her in the spring of a woman's life. And I mean, don't get me wrong, you'll find a similar explanation on Wikipedia. But it wasn't very nuanced, right?"

He tipped his chin, like he was full of incisive comments he just wasn't bothering to share because he was sure she'd already processed the same thoughts.

"Right. So all of that, and the high marks on my shunga research paper, aside, I latched on to this idea. Too much of art, across so many regions and traditions and eras, focuses on capturing that supposedly fleeting female beauty thing. So, it was around then that I pretty much stopped painting younger cis women, and focused on exploring the beauty—transient or not—of other people."

Abe cleared his throat, took another sip of his iced coffee, and spoke almost hesitantly. "That's kind of fascinating. And also, I guess, I never thought of myself as beautiful before."

She lifted the canvas a couple of inches, as if to say: Well, check out how wrong you are.

His cheeks went a bit red.

She found herself fighting those giggles again. "It's not that you're any more beautiful than anybody else. You're fine."

He snorted. Probably he'd noticed her checking him out in a non-artistic way.

"Yes, well. Point is, I'm not picking through people looking for the beautiful ones to paint. My models are a jumping off point for me to explore the beauty that's in everyone."

"Is that why you do the wings, as a metamorphosis sort of thing? Butterflies and chrysalises?"

She returned the painting to its stack. "No, not entirely, though there is a lot of cultural significance to butterflies. Representation of the soul of a person, sometimes a portent of a visit from a loved one—what you'd probably expect, and I'm not disavowing that in my work. But you know I've been painting since I was, like, two, right?"

He nodded. "I've heard."

"So, back before we moved to the States, someone gave me a book with all these photos of the flying insects of Japan. Lots of butterflies and beetles and moths and such like. And I just really liked trying to copy them, to draw and paint the wings especially. That's when I started to dislike watercolors, because I couldn't manage to render as much detail as I wanted in them. I switched to acrylics and moved on from there. Pretty much every medium I've ever worked in, I've learned by painting insects. My dad thought I'd end up as a scientific illustrator someday, but the science part never interested me. Just what I could do with a blank canvas and my imagination. It was actually a bit of a whim when I first added wings onto some of my figures. But once I did, they really took off."

He laughed, and she rolled her eyes. "I didn't mean that as a pun."

"And yet you managed."

"I guess I'd better add brilliant word play to my list of skills and accomplishments."

He stashed his drink and stood, shouldering his backpack. "Also add graciousness when accepting an apology. Thanks for letting me express it, and thanks for showing me the painting. Even if you did make me pretty damn worried about it for a minute there."

Now she really needed him to leave so she could send Alicia the most elaborate series of texts describing how she'd unveiled the painting to him. She handed over her now-empty flask. "Keep making me these cappuccinos, and I'll keep immortalizing every facet of your inner beauty."

"Hey, did you happen to see the most beautiful man on the beach," Noah crooned as Abraham walked up.

Austin and Alicia bent together to hide their grins, acting about as subtle as a screed on a conspiracy site. He refrained from bashing any of his relatives with his backpack as he swung it to rest on one of the blankets spread around the fire ring. He was mature like that.

"When do I get to see how the renowned artist reflected your larger than life glory?" Noah asked.

He shot a quelling look at his cousin, who ignored him.

Alicia answered him instead. "Callie will be happy to have you drop by to look, I'm sure. Mateo and I are taking her for a late brunch on Sunday if you want to swing by Saturn and meet her."

"Ohhh, migas and a gander at the woman who thinks our Abe here is worth immortalizing? Yes, please."

"Wait, you're going to brunch at Saturn and didn't invite me?" Austin flicked his bottle cap at Alicia. Mateo collected it in his recycling bag. "So rude."

Alicia rolled her eyes. "Aren't you on shift on Sunday?"

"Yeah, but I can make Abe trade with me."

"You already tried that when you wanted to schedule a date for Saturday," Abraham said. "Answers still no."

Austin was glaring firebolts at him, and it took Mateo's wide eyes and head tilt for Abraham to figure out why. Leyla had settled in next to Sally.

Right. Because God forbid Leyla become aware that Austin ever dated anyone. Not that he ever could muster up the guts to ask her out. He seemed to want her to never think of him and dating in any context.

His brother's hopeless crush aside, he still wasn't going to trade shifts. He was caving on Sunday.

He did his youngest sibling the kindness of telling Noah,

in the most neutral terms he could think up, about Callie's painting of him. It distracted everyone from the topic of who was going to brunch and who was working the cafe over the weekend. It also opened him up to approximately nineteen tons of bullshit masquerading as humor from his cousin. At one point, Noah actually demanded he start the description of the painting over, so he could record it in a voice memo to send to his sister.

He did not comply.

He was a nice person, so he also didn't turn the conversation back to who Austin was dating and who he wished he was dating, instead.

But then Noah pulled up an article about Callie and started looking between her photo and Abraham. He kept riffing about how he was starting to understand why Abraham was so eager to strip down for her, and how Callie was just Abraham's type, and how it must have revved his motor for the pretty artist to ask him for help, since being helpful was Abraham's catnip. It was too damn much.

He looked at Mateo. "Seriously. Tell me how to get my cousin to shut up."

Mateo raised his eyebrows. "Because suddenly you're the one whose personal life is a topic of conversation around bonfire? Guess what, friend, I am not sympathetic."

He thought back to the early phase of Mateo and Alicia turning their friends with benefits arrangement into something more permanent, and the number of times it was discussed around this very fire ring. The number of jokes he'd been in on, if not instigated outright.

So, okay, maybe he could understand part of Mateo's point.

"It's not like I'm dating Callie. I don't see why her painting me has to turn into this whole pile-on about my life."

Austin coughed *bullshit* into his hand.

He told his brother to fuck off, but given how loudly Mateo was laughing, he doubted anyone heard him.

They didn't have to understand his words for his point to be perfectly clear.

Chapter Thirteen

"Bye, all," Callie was saying as he approached her door. The steady stream of hangers-on had been trickling past him as he approached his own apartment. She started to shut her door behind the last of them, but opened it again when she saw him.

"Hey, Abraham."

Was she eying his backpack? Not that he expected her to understand his codes, or that the purple one was what he used to haul in his groceries and other shopping. So, no, he hadn't brought her another coffee.

He stopped anyway. "Hi. Work good?"

She nodded. "I think I'm getting somewhere. I guess that chat with you the other day really helped. Thanks for that."

"Sure, yeah. And, well, I was thinking. You're going to brunch tomorrow with Alicia and Mateo?"

"Yeah. I can't believe Saturn is still open and I haven't been there yet."

"It's an institution. Not just for the college crowd, either."

"Not every institution survived the past few years. I'm glad Saturn did."

"Same. Though my cappuccinos are better than theirs." He waited for, and enjoyed, the slight lift of her shoulders as she breathed out a smile. Bolstered, he went on. "I'm going caving in the morning."

"Oh, like you did that first time I met you? Something about a green slide?"

"Slope, but no. This is a different system. It starts a little higher up in the foothills. Lots of redwoods and ferns and things up there."

"Sounds nice. Except for the diving into the bowels of the earth part, of course."

His ears itched. "That's the thing. After you were talking about insects and stuff, I thought maybe you would like to come along. Check it out. Soak up the beauty and whatever."

"Oh."

Would that be her whole answer?

"I mean. I have that brunch ..."

He jumped in with embarrassing reassurances. Damn the bonfire crew for pointing out how obvious his crush on Callie was. "I know, but that's later. We'd be back by then. Even with enough time for you to take a shower or whatever before we— before you—head to Saturn."

"Do you want to come to brunch? Because that would be fine. It's just the whole slithering around in places where bats, snakes, lizards, and I don't know what other troglobites hang out that I'm not so keen on."

All of his weight had been balanced on his heels like he was ready for a quick getaway at any second. The fact she could name troglobites even as she rejected him? It somehow rebalanced him. "Right."

"Bears. Do they have bears up there? I know there are bears in California. Maybe cougars or leopards or wild boar?"

He couldn't help a short laugh. No wonder her art was so imaginative. She had wellsprings of creative thought. "I think you'll find that leopards are native to, like, sub-Saharan Africa. I've never had a dangerous animal encounter out there."

"Well, still. I know better than to put my genius brain at risk like you're suggesting. So, nice try, but I'm gonna keep to my lifelong practice of exploring animal life via photographs, thanks very much."

He nodded and gave in to the impulse to step back from her doorway. "Okay. It was just a thought."

"Still, though. Come to brunch afterwards if you'd like. That'd be nice."

And maybe she meant it, but he'd faced all the rejection he needed for the weekend.

Alicia asked for a table for three.

"Isn't your brother joining us?"

"No, he's got a shift this morning."

She cocked her head. "I thought he was caving."

"Oh, that brother." Alicia and Mateo exchanged a look.

"What?"

"Nothing. I didn't say anything. I've never said a thing in my entire life." She widened her eyes, like Callie might actually believe her innocent act.

Mateo gestured to the specials board. "You gotta try the Reuben here sometime. They use my high protein rye bread, and it pairs just beautifully with the corned beef and sauerkraut."

"Nice diversion," Callie said. "I'm totally distracted from the way you two were doing that couples thing of having silent conversations the rest of us aren't privy to."

Alicia offered Mateo a high five. "Good job, babe. We're killing this whole subtlety thing."

"You are the worst ever," Callie said.

Alicia wrinkled her nose. "That's what makes us so good together. Our collective worseness."

"Oh my god, so smug. Remind me why I thought it would be a good idea to go out with just the two of you?" Callie asked.

"You didn't. You thought Abe would be joining us." Her bestie smirked at her, and since she was, annoyingly, correct, Callie couldn't do anything to refute her.

It didn't stop her from making a face before latching onto Mateo's clever diversion strategy, asking him more about what things on the menu featured products from James Family Bakers. They let her get away with it. Good thing, because she was in no mood to get detailed about her reaction to Abraham not joining them for brunch.

They spent the meal exchanging bits of gossip she'd picked up since returning to Surfside, and hearing about some of the work Mateo was doing with the City Council. It was amusing to be the observer for once, while someone else was the constantly recognized one. She was used to being approached by strangers, but at Saturn, Mateo was the one the locals sought out.

Once they'd gotten their food, and she and Alicia had split their migas and crab cakes with each other, Mateo asked how her work was going.

"It's going," she said. "I could stand a little more inspiration, I suppose, but I'll get there."

"Huh," Alicia said.

"Meaning?" She didn't really want to ask, since four years of rooming with Alicia and countless hangs since meant she was plenty familiar with the woman's skeptical utterances.

It was getting so she could compile an entire lexicon of the Wells siblings' single syllable utterances. Fuck.

"I just think it's intriguing."

"What's intriguing?" Fuck, again, for opening herself to an opinion when she was raw.

"That you're looking for inspiration, when you already told me that you'd solved half your problems by knowing exactly what to make for Wolf."

"I mean, yes. Or—no. I've got a lot of the basics set up, sure, but it's been a little bit harder than I anticipated to start over like this." She dashed some habanero salsa over the migas. "It'll happen. I mean, I'm talented. We all know this."

"Clearly," Alicia agreed.

"And I'm always working at my art. No one can say I'm not dedicated."

"Furthest thing from my mind," Mateo chimed in. What a delightfully loyal guy he was.

"Right, so the thing is: I've got talent, and I've got drive. And I've got everything I need. So really, there's no point in me being kind of a mess about this. I should just be able to get on with it."

"So let's investigate that," Alicia said. Another local approached Mateo, so the two women edged closer to each other, lowering their voices. "Obviously we're starting from the premise that I love, adore, and admire you, and think you're the best."

"Obviously."

"But, okay. You've been making art pretty much your entire life."

"Right."

"And nobody can deny that this fire was more than enough to put you on the list of people who should never have to deal with bad stuff ever again. Especially if you factor in your tough transition when your family immigrated, and all that mean girl crap when you were older."

"Sign me up for this excellent-sounding list," she said.

"As soon as I find it, I will," Alicia promised. "But the

thing I'm thinking about is—you told me about the classes that you took, the trips to museums, the summer camps and all that."

"And fine arts high school." Even putting aside the hell of the transition, what with being the anointed one from day one and how that meant a thousand social cuts from people she'd thought would become a community of friends who understood her. She'd quickly had to learn to ignore their defensive scorn and focus only on the work.

"And that. So, I'm wondering if, when it comes to inspiration, you've always been spoilt for choice? I'm thinking you've been able to chase after anything that called out to you, and had the tools and the time you needed to really dig in. And that's amazing. I mean ... What a gift for your entire life. And a gift for the art world, that they get to enjoy the results," she added.

Callie laughed. She loved when Alicia got into the spirit of liberal praise. It was something she encouraged in everyone she knew who wasn't a straight white man, the application of liberal, unapologetic affirmations of self-worth and praise for themselves. And for her, too, while they were at it. She was an absolute leader in that way.

"Truer words. I'm pretty special. But, what I hear you saying is that I've had an easy time of it?"

Mateo turned back to the table. "I literally just heard her say you've had hardships."

"Okay, okay. Point taken. But in the arena of my work, my vocation?" Callie asked.

Alicia slipped bites of Mateo's crepe onto each of their plates. "Little bit of a silver platter, yeah. Not that you didn't have the talent and the dedication to take those gifts and turn them into your phenomenal, super well-deserved success. But your parents, your teachers, most of your fellow students—you've kind of been surrounded with support and encouragement and access and praise for almost thirty years."

"Ah," she said, because she could do single-syllable vocalizations, too. Also, because she was savoring the strawberry and Nutella goodness of Mateo's brunch.

Alicia raised her eyebrows.

Callie sighed. "Okay. Yes, fine. You continue to be insightful and brilliant, and are using your best friend powers only for good because you are a beautiful soul."

Mateo beamed at her. "I like you."

"As well you should. Your beloved has excellent taste in both friends and lovers," she said. They clinked their mimosas together.

Alicia joined in, then kissed them each on the cheek. "See, now? Aren't you glad my boring big brother didn't join us today? We'd never have gotten this deep dive into your psyche with him around."

Callie was too busy, thinking back over her entire artistic life, to take the time to disagree.

Chapter Fourteen

He hadn't known she was coming into the cafe.

She'd never done it before. Well, that one time when he made the first cappuccino for her. But she'd been holed up in her apartment most of the time since. Or at least, not in Pier Three, not while he'd been working downstairs.

In the weeks since Austin had converted the upstairs apartment, he'd grown to relish the expansiveness of spreading his work across the entire surface of the conference table, instead of shuffling everything while crowded at the desk in the cafe's joint office and storeroom. But there was a group booked into the conference suite, so Abraham had organized his receipts and invoices across the long table near the patio doors.

It was a glorious day and most of the customers were outside, or were taking their drinks to stroll down the beach or along the pier to spot the cavorting dolphins just offshore. He didn't feel like he was in the way. Besides, he owned the place. Or, a third of the place. If he wanted to take over an entire table for a couple of hours, who was going to complain?

Not Callie, apparently. She strolled in, glanced around as if processing criteria he couldn't begin to understand, and pulled out one of the chairs opposite him.

"This will work great. Can I?" Without even finishing the question, she shuffled half his piles to one side or the other so she could make room for her sketchpad. "Excellent."

He blinked at her. "In what way is this excellent?" He shifted the K through N invoices she'd just disarranged, putting them in line with the K through N packing lists.

"Because the light is beautiful, and the space lets me spread out, and I already know you can sit there for like two whole hours without making a sound to disturb me. Plus, it looks like this table is nice and solid and won't go skittering across the room if somebody nudges you again."

He grunted, because whether she meant to or not, she amused him.

Baptiste called her to the counter to get her drink. When she returned, he couldn't stick to her implied request for silence. "That's not a cappuccino."

"Wow, I can tell that you really are the owner of a coffee shop with astute observations like that." She didn't elaborate about her choice of an espresso and tonic.

He let it go. Went back to tallying the expense categories of the accounts payable.

She didn't ask, but he paused to consolidate more of his paperwork so she had room to spread out her various supplies. From the way she positioned herself, facing the patio and the ocean beyond, he expected her to maybe be drawing a landscape or seascape or something.

Instead, her sketching seemed to be clusters of people spread out at tables, but rather than rolling waves behind them, she was roughing in what looked like boulders or a mountain. She added a fern that loomed over the tables, and some wings to the coffee drinkers.

"Is that ... are they?" He didn't know quite what to ask.

Callie took a sip of her drink, puckered her lips, and ignored him. He collected the A through J paperwork and delivered it to his office. Before returning to the table, he stopped behind the counter to blend up a couple of cappuccinos. He dropped hers at her elbow before skirting the table with his own.

She'd added in more shading above the people/bugs, and made them surface below the tables rough with scattered rocks or dirt. The distinctive vertical strips of bark on the tree that grew from the ground above them clearly indicated it was a redwood.

"It's a cave." He didn't know if he was asking, or stating it.

At that, she looked up and noticed the second drink. "I wish I knew why this is so much better than every other drink I try now."

He wriggled his eyebrows at her. "A man's got to have some mystery to keep you intrigued."

Her smile slid into something smug. "So you want me to be intrigued?"

He could let her keep playing her constant bantering games, or he could lay it on the line.

Maybe she was such a naturally sunny and playful and confident person that everyone fell under her sway, and there was nothing unusual to her about the vibe between them. But for him, when he got close to her, the air bounced with possibility.

And somehow, she got him talking, volunteering more about himself than was typical. Even though he was just as content to sit back and listen to what she had to say.

Fuck it. If she was this magnetically appealing to everyone else, she was probably used to people confessing their attraction. Hopefully he wouldn't disconcert her. And she'd been the one to approach him, when he'd been working silently alone, so that could be a positive indication.

If she shut him down, he'd retreat. But she'd given him an opening, so he took it. "I wouldn't mind if you're a bit intrigued by me, since I am by you."

He watched her carefully, not missing the warm flash of her eyes.

When she didn't answer, he said, "I can back off if you want."

She curled one leg up onto the chair and wrapped her arm around it. "Did I say I wanted?"

"No, but you did turn me down when I asked you out."

Her brows pinched together. "When did you ask me out?"

"On Saturday."

"When you tried to lure me underground? I thought that was just a casual offer."

"It was more than that. I mean, I meant it to be." He reached for printouts he'd folded into his back pocket. "Here, by the way. I took some photos on Sunday so you could see what caves are like without getting spiders in your hair."

She immediately began flipping through the images. "This is ..." She looked up with a wide smile.

"You said you like working with pictures."

She rifled through the stack, extracting a shot of the cave entrance and laying it beside her sketchpad. Her fingers skittered over what she'd drawn as she compared the two. With visible effort, she tore her gaze away and turned the printouts face down on top of her work. "Sorry. We were discussing how bad you are at asking people out on dates."

He couldn't suppress a laugh. "Were we?"

"Oh, yeah you're terrible at it. You keep showing up over and over again with some sort of highly addictive caffeine, and then threatening me with bats and snakes."

"Don't forget the jaguars."

"And jaguars. Exactly. Did you never consider just saying,

'Hey, Callie, you are spectacular, and I want to get to know you better? How about we go out to dinner?'"

It was the most Callie thing he'd could imagine. He fell even deeper into his intrigue over her.

She stared him down, sending one of her pencils twirling up and over each of her knuckles as she waited.

He shook his head, because there was no getting around how driven he was to take this chance. "Callie Hamasaki, you are incredible. Allow me, please, to take you to dinner so I can spend an evening becoming further amazed by you."

Chapter Fifteen

Austin caught him in the middle of unpacking and repacking his red backpack. "Oh, hey, whoa. So, this is why you switched shifts to have Wednesday morning off."

First time in recorded history the kid remembered which backpack was which. He fumbled the condoms to the floor. He'd been checking the expiration date on them when his brother barged in.

Before he could get there, Austin swooped forward and scooped them up, making a mock pitying face at the packaging. "Well, we can't all need extra-large. I'm sure it's the motion of the ocean anyway." And then the brat patted him on the shoulder condescendingly, because apparently, he wanted Abraham to lurch at him and wrestle him to the ground. It was a satisfying few minutes before they both collapsed against his bed.

"You know," Austin said, "it's really a damn good thing we don't live with Mom and Dad anymore. They'd claim it's wrong of us to still be wrestling as much as we do."

"It's a perfectly reasonable way to get some exercise and to burn off some frustration."

"Yeah, you try telling our folks that. They'd just lecture about," Austin waved his hand, "all that fraternal feeling bull-shit they love to go on about."

Abe knocked his knee into Austin's. "One of these days they'll accept that we're never going to be friends."

"I live in hope, big bro. Who's your date with?"

He grunted.

"Interesting. That's quite a clue. So, she lives in the building?"

He smacked his left arm across his brother's chest.

"Hey, ow, man. You're going to bruise me with that thing."

"Don't take your shirt off around Mom and Dad, then, or I'll get in trouble."

"You think they still recognize a prosthetic shaped bruise?"

He held up the arm. He'd quickly twisted off the terminal device before flattening his brother to the floor, but his carbon fiber forearm still packed a punch. Or it would, if they weren't both too aware of not damaging it to bring it into the tussle. "Wouldn't put it past them."

Austin did one of his yoga-inspired moves, scissoring up into a V shape before standing.

"Show off."

"Don't hate me because I'm graceful. Hate me because I'm also beautiful and strong. Have fun with Callie tonight."

With that, the brat left, leaving Abraham in need of a shower before he could finish packing up and heading out for his date.

She was caught in a memory lane cul-de-sac about her dating life when she lived in Surfside for college. Mostly she'd been a casual dater: a month or so with one guy, a beat or two of nothing, then dating someone else a few times. Never too serious or committed.

It was easier to do casual enjoyment. To have a few fun times, instead of getting all caught up in the need to spend every spare moment with some guy. Alicia would often tease her about her low-key vibe, but she figured nobody could ever mean as much to her as her painting.

She had a romantic side. Not just the part of her that enjoyed hot guys and going out dancing and flirting and all that, but also—she wasn't immune to, for example, the way her stomach fluttered when Abraham gave her a stack of photos he'd taken just for her. Or the way he paused a beat before parroting back her request for a date in his own sincerely uttered words.

So, yeah, maybe she didn't have a bunch of relationship experience under her belt, but she did plan on enjoying whatever this turned out to be with Abraham.

Just as soon as she figured out what to wear for their date.

He was on time. Given that he lived about twenty-two feet from her, it wasn't surprising, but she still found herself charmed by it.

Not the most subtle indication about whether her emotions were invested in this whole dating thing.

"You look great." He handed her a bouquet already in a vase. "It needs water. I didn't want to spill."

She carefully tipped it into the sink, stroking free a spot for the faucet to reach the lip. "Thanks. I recognize the fern and lupine. What's this other one?"

"Wild pea. And the yellow ones are California poppy."

She turned it to catch sight of the bursts of deep cadmium yellow among the lavender and violet shades of the pea and lupine. It was all set off in a wild and almost turbulent way by the feathery oxide green fronds of lady fern.

"This is so fun. I adore it. Did you pick all these?"

He rubbed his left arm. He wasn't wearing a prosthetic and the sleeve of his Henley was pushed up on both sides to clear his elbows. "I did. I would have gone to a florist, but after you liked the pictures, I thought you'd like to see what kinds of thing I find when I'm out hiking or caving. It's past bloom season for a lot of wildflowers, but these were still plentiful."

She traced the closely packed blooms of the lupine. Most of the stems were in the purple range, but one was such a subtle shade it read as white. "You were right. I'm glad you brought the outdoors in to me. But don't mistake my pleasure for a desire to crawl through your beloved caves."

"You've been clear."

"Excellent. I love the shirt by the way. Did you read something about how the Henley is the sexiest shirt on a guy, or is it just part of your habitual rugged wardrobe?"

The cream shirt paired well with his dark jeans and the russet bag slung over his shoulder. And with the blush on his cheeks.

"I, um, thanks."

She did love playing with him. She leaned in and kissed one of those red cheeks, just above his beard and ever so close to his lips. "You're not doing a good job at hiding your sweet side, Abraham Wells."

He caught her up and brought their bodies flush and their foreheads together. "You're not doing a great job encouraging me to leave this apartment so I can feed you, Callie Hamasaki."

He took her to a place she'd not heard of, over on the Pier One edge of town. Abraham explained he'd discovered it through the work Alicia and Mateo were doing to unify local businesses and encourage people living in and visiting Surfside to support those enterprises.

"I've been here a couple of times. Pork chops are my favorite so far. Oh, and do you drink? The wine list is great."

"So, this is what it's like to be romanced by you?"

He sat back all casual like he didn't know what she was talking about.

"You unleash your practiced patter, telling me about all the good you do in the world, and wait for me to swoon."

"I ..." He cleared his throat, and she could see him fighting back denials. He absolutely did not want to admit that he had game.

She knew guys like this. Clearly, she secretly adored guys like this. Stoic, and somehow abashed. Like it would never occur to them their dates might question if they do the exact same thing with every new person they take out.

Why was she like this? Why was it so fun to tease that hint of vulnerability to the forefront, when it was clear he'd rather hide it and act like he was beyond any nerves at the situation? Well, good luck with that, Abraham Wells. She bit back a contented little smile that must have still shown in her eyes, from the way he was looking all wary at her.

She gave him a bit of a reprieve. "I do drink, but you can't count on me for a half bottle of wine. You better go into it knowing that I'm not pulling equal weight here."

He grabbed hold of her subject change lifeline. "Would you prefer a cocktail, or beer? Their draft list isn't bad."

She skimmed the menu. "No, wine. Dry red. I'm getting the brisket and the truffle mac."

"You're the boss." He set aside the wine list.

After ordering, she looked around. "So you didn't know this place at all before Alicia's website thing?"

"I'd heard of it, yeah, but never been. I'll admit I've got a couple of go-to places for dinner dates."

"You date a lot?"

He blushed. Damn sweet man. "I'm not always as bad at expressing my interest as I was with you."

She shouldn't but she wanted to ask what kept him in

check with her. Probably not the sister's friend thing. None of the Wells's seemed the type to let potential messiness stop them. After all, Mateo had been not only a family friend, but a business connection, and part of their larger friend group. None of that had stopped Alicia from hooking up with him for months before she caught feelings. Or before she admitted to catching them, anyway.

But if she teased a bit more about his too-subtle expressions of interest, she'd end up tripping over her own reluctance to name things. The Wells trio could be as up front and messy as they liked. But it wasn't the Hamasaki way to go digging up identifiers for her tender emotions.

Seeing the chef through the window to the kitchen, she grabbed for a subject change. "Is this a Black-owned business?"

Abraham looked around and caught the chef's eye. They tipped acknowledging chins at each other. "It is. Dante's aunt is the owner. He's been head chef for a few years now, and his cousin is the manager."

She pulled out her phone, and was looking up the Keep Surfside Swell website that Alicia and Mateo and their friends had set up to highlight locally-owned businesses. She tapped on the restaurant and checked the links. "Why don't you mention that?"

"What do you mean?"

She showed him the screen. "This has all of the businesses, and you even list ones that are multigenerational, like here and the bakery. But nothing highlights the businesses that are minority-owned. Or woman-owned, for that matter."

"Is that important, for the mission of the campaign, that is? I mean, I guess it must be since you mentioned it?"

"Listen to you, trying not to say anything screwed up because you're dating a woman who's also a minority."

"Hey, I'm not trying to downplay. I'm not good at discussing this, maybe?"

"What, that you're a white man living in a white man's world?"

He shrugged, and she tilted her head, wondering if he was going to point out his left arm. To his credit, he didn't. At least not as an initial defense. "The thing is, I know you know all this, because when you all took your inheritance and set up Pier Three Coffee, you committed to making it a wealth-building enterprise for people who are traditionally less likely to come from families with wealth to pass on to their grand-children."

"That's what we're doing with the wage structure, and the profit sharing."

"Right, I know, and that's commendable. So is this campaign." She tapped her cell phone. "From an inclusion standpoint, it hits all the marks. And so does what you're doing with Pier Three. And what Mateo is doing with the City Council's wage initiative and everything. Don't misunderstand me—wealth equity work is important."

Their food arrived. She topped up their wine glasses.

"But the thing about access is, Black- and minority-owned businesses have always had—still have—systemic barriers in place. It's not just redlining, or underfunded schools, affecting people's personal and educational lives. There's too long a history of discrimination against Black and minority owners in banking, in access to raw goods, in getting favorable terms with vendors. It's that kind of access gap that I bet means the proportion of businesses on the Swell list that are owned by BIPOC people is lower than the overall demographics of Surf-side. You can't just list them in with everybody else and call it inclusion. You have to acknowledge that the hurdles are differ-ent, and smooth out the road."

He pierced a chunk of the pork chop that came out of the kitchen pre-sliced at his request. "I know about hurdles."

"Of course you do. Mateo is a queer Mexican-American, and Alicia is a woman. None of you have gone into any of this without thinking about the world in more inclusive ways than the average guy. But something Alicia said to me the other day about the way I've always had support got me thinking." She graced him with a smile. "This is delicious, by the way."

<h1 style="text-align:center">Chapter Sixteen</h1>

He glanced at her meal, which did look like a savory wonderland. But he was beginning to feel combative, and needed to defuse himself and sit with the discomfort of her insights. So he asked a question, to keep her talking, and to help keep his own mouth shut. "What did my sister say?"

"Nothing about you, or Surfside. We were talking about me."

He welcomed the hint of humor in her tone. After one too many experiences of her self-aggrandizement, it was feeling a bit too sincere when she said that stuff. Not that he had anything against self-confidence, and it was clear she'd earned the professional accolades, but it was a little relief to sense that she could tell she bragged on herself a lot.

"I was bemoaning my work for not going the way I want. And the fact that Wolf was expressing reservations. She reminded me that I've always had so many support systems. My family, most of all, but also my teachers. Opportunities. The means to explore my art."

"But you've also got the talent."

"Oh, sure, I could have had all those other things and

ended up with a few cute paintings on my parents' guest bedroom wall, or selling at the occasional local fair. I've got talent, and I've honed it, but plenty of people have as much talent and drive as I do, and the street fair booth is about where their artistic endeavors will stop. Maybe they didn't have the lessons, camps, and international trips featuring long hours in art museums like I did. Maybe they didn't have a college fund, the determination, the mentorship, and the know-how that I did to jump on all those early opportunities I got being on campus with access to people who could help me go wider. But that's my point. It's that all that stuff made my path here relatively smooth. Yes, it was uphill, but it wasn't riddled with pot holes or obstructed by boulders. And I had, I don't know, a fuel efficient four wheel drive vehicle that was fully paid up. You three, you had your grandmother's inheritance, as well as your various skill sets, as well as being white, and having parents who are business owners to give you good advice. And probably mentors from your education or previous work experience as well."

He wanted to shake his head, but it would be a false denial. She was spot on about it all. He emptied his wine glass instead.

She took a band off her wrist, using it to tie her long dark hair back in a low ponytail.

He got distracted by the candlelight on the exposed length of her neck. The birthmark he wanted to kiss. The way her eyelashes fluttered over her cheeks while she arranged her asparagus in a pattern over her mac and cheese. But not so distracted that he missed her point about other artistic people not having her resources. Or other business owners, to be more pointed about her point, not having the institutional advantages that he and his siblings did.

Abe offered her the last of the wine. She waved him off.

He poured it for himself. "We did talk about this when we were setting up Pier Three."

"I know you did," she said, and the candlelight sparking on her eyes was even more entrancing than that on her neck. "Alicia talked a lot about all that, when we were designing Pier Three's interior. And like I said, I completely respect that. But, Abraham, that was years ago now. I know the Surfside Swell campaign had a lot to do with getting your financing for the building, and a bunch of the beneficial side effects grew from there. It seems like you're not thinking beyond what's already been done. I'm not denying what you've accomplished, or saying everything has to come from a place of pure altruism. But I don't get why you've just stopped the process of your thinking. Don't you want to grow beyond the point where you are now, and see what else might be possible?"

Abraham felt like he was staring blankly at her. He turned his attention to his mashed potatoes, hoping time would help him formulate an answer. Maybe she was right, and they were stuck. He'd never have said so, but when did saying something make it true? He wasn't so naive as to believe she might not have a point.

Taking out his own phone, he typed a note to contact Quinn to ask about adding minority-owned business designations to the website.

"Are you offended?"

He flashed her a smile. "Are you worried about my fragile white male ego?"

Her face said that maybe, yeah, she had been, but had no inclination to admit it. Which was good, because it meant he could pretend he hadn't been forced to contemplate his outdated thinking and knee jerk defensiveness. Goddamn societal conditioning always getting in the way of letting him have a good time on his dates.

"Okay, you're off the hook," she said. "Have you ever had

dessert here?"

For as much as she seemed to love teasing him, and her frequent insouciance, Abraham liked that she felt comfortable expressing such genuine thoughts.

And that she felt comfortable challenging him about them.

No doubt about it, Callie Hamasaki appealed to him on dozens of levels. He hoped they'd have a genuine chance to explore many of those levels beyond just this night.

They managed the rest of the meal without questioning each other's morals or intentions, which Callie was counting as a win. She wasn't sure what it prompted her to even start the conversation about equity and access, except that she really had been mulling it over since her brunch with Alicia and Mateo. She put a halt to all that, though, and so did he. They focused on enjoying their meal, and each other. At least, she assumed that was what he was doing. It definitely was what she was up to, and probably she wasn't very subtle about eyeing him.

He was watching her as blatantly as she was watching him.

Probably all the heat between them had started that first day in Surfside, when he brought the gang to her door. His face had been such a picture of disapproval that she longed to draw him. The urge got even stronger once he'd returned from his caving expedition and consented to pose for her.

If she could call it consent when she'd hardly offered him a choice.

"What are you smiling about?"

"I'm remembering how happy you were to pose for me for my *Heart Wings / Heartstrings* portrait."

"I thought you were calling it something to do with

moths?"

"Haven't decided for sure. I've got time before Wolf needs me to give him titles for the show."

"How does that work?"

"How does what work?"

"You just deliver him the things, and people buy them and take them home?"

"By 'things' do you mean my artwork?"

"Well, yeah, of course. Your paintings and everything."

"Just paintings. My sketches and studies aren't for sale. I like to archive all that stuff." She frowned. "Which I guess means I like to archive all that stuff now, since I lost most of the work notebooks I used to have."

"I suppose it's not the kind of thing you can have electronic backups of."

"Not entirely. I do post a good bit as part of my social media presence. And for commissions, I usually have an email discussion, with scans, to work out the details and direction before I start painting."

"It's probably not the same as having your stack of notebooks, though." His voice was sympathetic, but not pitying, which Callie super appreciated.

She'd received so much sympathy and kindness since the fire. Even the agent for her renter's insurance was super accommodating and solicitous while they sorted out her damages. But everyone inevitably went overboard with their pity.

She wanted to appreciate their generosity, but without letting them pity her and, annoyingly, pouring out their own tales of woe. Like whatever losses they'd had could mitigate hers. It was exhausting by the end of day one of her post-fire life. Callie wasn't a super rude person, but it too often took too much effort to shut down those sympathetic noises she needed muted from her life, so she could go back to operating like somebody with an actual future ahead of her.

"What's the grim look for?" he asked, seemingly unbothered by her expression even as he was curious about it. "Was asking about the stuff you lost too much of a downer during this dinner where we've gotten along so famously and effortlessly?"

His teasing hit the mark, and she found herself laughing away her contemplative mood. "Okay, no more navel gazing. Tell me why exactly you think burying yourself underground is a jolly pastime?"

She managed to not pump her fist when she tripped him into talkativeness again. At some point whenever he got chatty with her, his brow would wrinkle like he couldn't figure out how it happened.

"Okay, first of all, I'm not being buried underground. I emerge every time."

She pounced. "So far. It only takes one primordial bat to attack you and drag you deep into her lair, and poof, you're never to be heard from again."

He scoffed. "Bats do not have lairs. That's bears. Bears have lairs; bats roost in trees. Or, okay, in caves, but not in a lair-type system."

"Nice try, Mr. Nature, but you're still not selling this whole caving experience."

He considered her over the last of his wine. "If I do sell it, are you saying you'd come with me sometime?"

She made a face but didn't shoot him down.

"There's a good beginner's cave up on the other side of campus, in the foothills. Not the one those photos are from, but near it. You could even stand upright in most of the chambers."

"Chambers," she repeated with a dramatic shudder, wondering if it was a good cover for the shiver she experienced when she realized she'd been tallying just how many times she'd made him laugh.

Chapter Seventeen

They kissed at her door.

After dinner, he'd introduced her to Escubac and tonic. She'd enjoyed the subtle botanicals and citrus hints in the digestif, but a little booze went a long way with her. Abraham's tolerance seemed higher, but she'd caught a hint of unsteadiness as he stood, and that reminded her of exactly how little of the wine she'd consumed from their shared bottle.

He'd agreed readily enough to let her drive them back.

After a quick lesson in his car's adaptive turn signals, he left her to guide them back to the apartment complex. His silence, and the dark and quiet streets, and the just-long-enough drive back to their building gave her more than enough time to contemplate some stuff wriggling at the back of her mind. Like how much she was enjoying life in Surfside again. And how her date was her best friend's brother so she'd potentially be running into him for the rest of her life.

How he seemed to be fairly interested in getting physical with her.

All of Callie's long-term planning was based on growing

her career. Inasmuch as she'd factored in a personal life, she'd figured it would slot in around her professional goals, the way her dating life had to date. But it struck her, over the course of their date, that getting physical with Abraham might turn into a situation where her personal life impinged on her professional one.

It seemed like the kind of thing she should undertake with a bit of forethought. And maybe that he should, too. And after all he'd consumed at dinner, she couldn't know for sure Abraham's sober thoughts about sex and the future. So when they got to her door, she squeezed his hand to stop him. Their fingers had been interlaced since the parking lot, when she'd returned his keys.

He squeezed back, stepping just close enough to send tingles along her arms.

"So, that was fun." She pulled him closer. He smelled of all those botanical things from the liqueur, and also of the ocean, and also of coffee.

He probably always smelled of coffee.

Alicia had a separate laundry bag for her Pier Three clothes, because it was impossible to fully launder out the cafe scents from her work attire. Callie doubted that Abraham bothered to sort his own wash. But coffee smelled good on him, so she wasn't complaining.

"I like that smile on you," he said.

She gave up trying to distract herself from anything but the feel of him in front of her. "I like your arm around my waist."

"Yeah?" He hauled their bodies closer. Close enough for his heat to radiate in the scant space between them. All the giddy things were happening in her torso again, and she opted to obey the demands of her body. She laced her arms around his neck and tilted at him until their lips met.

It was fireworks her rib cage could hardly contain, and the

pressure of his lips and his chest as he urged their bodies closer. The slight brush of his beard and mustache as he wasted no time exploring her lips, her cheek. Her mouth again. The delicate yet intent dance of interaction.

They opened to each other, and the sound he made was between a groan and a growl. She felt explosions of all the dark and deep and intense and primal values—violet and magenta and phthalo turquoise—dancing behind her closed eyes.

She grasped to anchor a hand on his neck, ran the other over his cheek and shoulder and chest.

He pulled back, just a fraction. "Sorry, did you mind?"

She shook her head. "Mind what?" Not the kiss. He couldn't possibly think she minded the kiss. She didn't mind his tongue, she didn't mind the way he was gripping their bodies close, she didn't mind, not even a little, the hefty bulge in his pants.

He nodded to his left, to where she was gripping his tricep. "Are you pulling my arm back?"

"No?" And then it occurred to her that his stump was wrapped over her shoulder.

"It's not bothering you?" His question was a bit combative and a bit wary, but also a bit teasing and hopeful.

She thumped her head against his chest. "We already covered the fact that the Henley is sexy."

He ducked to meet her eye. "Are you calling me sexy?"

She turned to kiss his upper arm, tracing a path up his pecs and neck until she was nuzzling the underside of his beard. "Don't get full of yourself. Just because you kiss like you invented it and fill out a shirt well doesn't mean I'm swayed here."

"You're not, huh?" He caught her mouth again, like it was his mission to explore every nuance of how their lips and tongues fit together. It was goddamn unfair how well he kissed.

When they parted, she slumped against her door. "Okay, maybe a little swayed."

He ran a hand over his bag's strap. "I've got some supplies in here."

Wow. She'd never been literally taken aback before. She burst out laughing. "You live two doors down and you still packed for tonight? Pretty ballsy there, Wells."

"Prepared. I like to be prepared."

She wanted to strip the bag from him. To dig inside and see what he thought was so essential he'd carried it to the restaurant and back. But she also didn't want to ignore her earlier resolve to talk about physical stuff when he'd had less to drink. "Right, then, Mr. Sea Scout, the only thing you need to be prepared for is to say goodnight."

His nostrils flared and he bit his cheek, but he also stepped back from her. "If that's your call. Of course."

"It is. But maybe we can get together again soon?"

Abraham nodded, his posture relaxing some. "I'd really like that, Callie. That and more, to be clear."

She glanced down at his crotch. Licked her lips. "It's clear."

He palmed his face and groaned.

Callie stroked his arm again. "And you should know it's clear on my side, too. Now go away, so I can start imagining what I'm missing."

He leaned in for one last, hard, brief kiss, stroked her cheek, and walked away.

Chapter Eighteen

When he made his way into Pier Three at noon, he found his siblings hanging out behind the counter. Slipping on an apron, he went to join them. Without bothering to ask, Austin reached for the strings.

He swatted him away. "Don't treat me like a baby." It was what he learned to say as a kid, before he could remember the word *infantilize* from one day to the next. So it was what he still said if he thought his family was treating him differently because of his arm.

Austin's eyes widened, even as he stepped back and apologized. "Rude of me. Sorry."

He let it go with a sigh. It wasn't really Austin's fault. He and Alicia had grown up from day one with the expectation that they'd make Abraham's life easier. He'd been maybe eight when he noticed that his parents no longer cut up his siblings' meals into bite-sized pieces. Four-year-old Austin had a knife and fork, and so did six-year-old Alicia. But despite the prosthetic he wore pretty much constantly back then, he only had a fork.

Their parents had been perfectly conciliatory about his

demands for a knife of his own. But even at eight, he noticed that most of their meals for the next few days were ones that were easy to eat one handed. Maybe he couldn't remember how to say infantilization, but he could call out the casseroles with the reminder that his occupational therapist said no one was supposed to baby him.

It was that next Christmas that Austin received a kid-sized tool chest of his own, which he toted around the complex whenever his dad or the super had maintenance and repairs to complete. Austin had always been fascinated by that stuff, was the explanation he got when Abraham wondered why no one offered to teach him how to safely replace an electrical outlet or snake a clogged drain.

It was plausible. Everything was always plausible with his family, up to and including the point when he moved back to Surfside after grad school. It was around the same time Austin dropped out of undergrad, and their parents suggested the brothers take a two-bedroom apartment in the building. The super had recently moved on, and they told Abraham they hoped giving the job to Austin would anchor him a bit to an adult life.

Despite Austin's tendency to be a slob, Abraham liked living with him. In a lot of ways, he felt most himself around his brother. It was a balm for the festering feeling that his parents had engineered them living together so Abraham would always have somebody to look out for him, and make his life easier.

"You got home earlier than expected yesterday," Austin said. "I thought maybe you and Callie ..." He glanced at Alicia and trailed off.

"You thought he and Callie would what?" Alicia asked, arms crossed and eyes narrowed.

"Would wander the pier for a while."

Abraham snorted. Austin wasn't even trying to sound plausible.

Alicia turned her laser eyes on him. "Do you think he's funny?"

"I haven't thought he was funny one day in his entire life."

"Hey." Austin whapped the back of his head, knocking off his ball cap.

"Hey yourself." He hip-checked his brother as he bent to retrieve it.

"You two are such children. Could you maybe not egg each other on for ten minutes?"

"Eggs." He turned to Austin. "Add eggs to the shopping list."

"Because suddenly we don't have the same grocery app?" Austin grumbled, but complied.

"If you're quite done sorting out your domestic and romantic lives," Alicia said, "can we talk about our business?"

He definitely spent too much time with his siblings. Shame he loved them both so much.

They chatted about a couple of staffing and vendor issues while they worked, and once they'd ironed out a few things, he asked if Quinn would be at bonfire that week.

"They haven't said any different. Why?" Alicia asked.

"It's this idea Callie mentioned at dinner, about the Surfside Swell site," he started, only to field a snarky interruption from his brother.

"You spent your date talking about local business initiatives? No wonder you got back to your lonely bed so quickly."

"Quit sexualizing my best friend," their sister said. Which was Abraham's sentiment exactly.

Or, at least, he wanted any sexualizing of Callie to be a thing between just the two of them.

"Anyway, she suggested we add a widget, or whatever it would need to be, to the site to highlight Black- and minority-owned places. I want to ask Quinn what they'd need to implement that."

"Hang on." Alicia was scrolling on her phone like she'd see some obvious button he and Callie had overlooked. "I can't … we really don't have that already?"

"We really don't."

"It's a good idea," Austin said.

"Of course it's a good idea," she muttered, then glared at them. "We should have done that from the beginning. I'm mortified we didn't."

"If it makes you feel better, Callie said you're the one who inspired her to think about it. Well, you and the fact I took her to Lucille's last night."

"I'm not sure it does, actually. But how did I inspire her?"

He told her about how her brunch conversation had gotten Callie thinking about privilege and access, and how that expanded to their conversation about the Surfside Swell site.

"See, this is why she's my best friend," Alicia said. "Instead of blowing me off or getting defensive about it, she trusted me to be saying something worth hearing. Even though I obviously didn't mean to hurt her by saying it."

"I don't know for sure, but I don't think she was hurt."

"See, she's amazing. It's like she's got no ego sometimes."

He laughed, but he got what Alicia meant. It wasn't about Callie's self-esteem. It was about her way of viewing the world almost as a work in progress that she could—and would—positively impact.

He was wowed by how she did that so consistently, at least from what he knew of her so far. And it wasn't that he never encountered that strain of optimistic determination before. He'd been friends with Mateo for years now.

"So, well, if we don't catch Quinn at bonfire, we'll track them down Saturday," Alicia said.

"I'm caving on Saturday."

"I feel sure I can convey this message on my own." Alicia rolled her eyes, but hugged them both as she headed out. "See you tomorrow, big bro, little bro. Behave yourselves until then."

Normally, that was the kind of admonition aimed at Austin. But Abraham had the strong impression that, this time, she had been very distinctly speaking to him.

Salt messaged to see if she was up for company, and without thinking too much about it, Callie told him no.

Much as she generally liked having company around while she worked, she'd gotten into a rhythm that was going really well. She wasn't in the mood to mess with success.

Maybe she'd have to spend more time kissing Abraham Wells, since she'd come in after that date and spent the next three or four hours paging through her notebooks, refining sketches and altering her plan for Wolf's gallery.

She hadn't exactly gotten around to sleeping until almost four in the morning, but she'd been at her easel by ten, everything laid out according to her new plan for how to fix the small canvases. She'd been blazing through them since, laying the undercoat on two at time while she bopped around singing to her playlist.

She was getting shit done, and she was damn proud of it. It was the kind of work that left her feeling giddy and a little awed about what she was capable of. It secured her knowledge that her talent deserved to be celebrated. And the show she was crafting for The Wolfgang Lewis Gallery would ensure exactly that kudos.

Salt and whoever else wanted to watch her work, would just have to wait for another day.

She was pretty freaking immersed, so she didn't really notice the knock on her door until it got louder, and she realized she'd been incorporating the rapping into her little painting dance, as her mom had once called it. She shimmied over to the door and found Abraham standing there with drink in hand.

"It might be too late for caffeine for you. But I worked the closing shift today so I couldn't bring you a cappuccino earlier."

She realized she was still bouncing along to EXO and gentled her body. "That's all right."

"You're busy."

She pulled him through the door. "You have coffee. I'm not that busy."

He laughed and accepted her invitation. "Sure it's not too late?"

"Not even a little bit. I was up half the night working on this stuff." She waved at what might look like a mess of papers and canvases behind her. "I'm pretty sure I haven't had anything to eat yet today."

His smile grew. "Lucky for you, I picked up my own dinner on the way home."

"How is that lucky for me?"

"Well, I guess it does depend on if you like banh mi or not."

"Okay, tell me who you know that does not like banh mi."

"Austin. He hates cilantro and says even if I take it off it ruins the sandwich. That's why I get it. It means I can leave any leftovers in my fridge and he won't eat them."

"You're saying your brother's loss is my gain?"

"It would appear so."

"And you're resigned to life without the leftovers?"

He shrugged. "I'd rather share with you."

Never mind that she was probably going to get India

yellow on his Pier Three shirt. She just had to kiss him. She leaned in to keep as much as her smock as possible from touching him, and planted her lips on his.

After a brief break to clean up, she sank into the chair opposite him at her dining table. He'd already shuffled her work into a slightly neater pile and drawn the sandwiches out of his backpack.

"That's at least the third bag I've seen you carry. Isn't it a pain to change them out all the time?" She was definitely a one bag until it fell apart kind of person.

"It's a system. This one, the black, is my work bag." He set his water bottle on the table and offered her the choice of pork or tofu sandwich.

"Go halfsies?"

He nodded and she arranged the switch. "Thanks for this. Oh. Hang on, before we get jalapeño breath." She rounded the little table and scratched her fingers through his hair as he tilted his chin up to her mouth. She slipped into his lap as he scooched back his chair, and she leaned into his lovely chest as they kissed.

She said, "This is nice. I should maybe make a habit of feeling up the chests of people I paint in future. It's a lot of fun."

"I don't want to tell you how to approach your artistic process, but I will volunteer to be your only model for a while, if that's what you decide." His hand skimmed over her shoulder and down her side, coming to rest on her hip. "Alternately, if it gets me access to you, I might have to learn how to wield a brush myself."

He hadn't touched her anywhere intimate yet, but she could practically feel the pressure of his hand cupping her breast, just from how much she thought it would be a great idea. Of course, it was also a good idea to attend to some of her body's other cravings, like hunger and thirst.

One last squeeze to his shoulders and she slid away. "You're too tempting. Quit distracting me from my food."

"If I hadn't shown up, how long would you have gone before stopping to feed yourself?"

She twisted her lips as she finished a bite of the scrumptious sandwich. "Probably not more than an hour? I don't usually go a full day without eating, though come to think of it, I did have a couple of apples last night. So, thank you for the meal."

She braced herself for the kind of lecture that disguised itself as concern over the way she chose to live in her own damn body. She'd known Alicia, and Katherine Wells, for years now, so she shouldn't have been surprised that instead, he said, "We carry a few shelf stable snack packs at Pier Three. If you want, I can bring you some to keep by your easel. That way you'll be able to grab them quick if you're too focused on your work to get up."

Points for the Wells family right there. She'd have to thank Katherine for raising kids who understood not to police other people's choices. "I feel like I'm going to put Pier Three out of business with all the stuff you keep feeding me."

"Eh. We factor in a certain amount for employee consumption. I'm just bringing mine to you instead of eating it myself."

"Seems like that's against the principles of good accounting."

Abe shrugged. "It's like with my bags. I've got a system that works. I don't see why I should try to change it."

"No, indeed. Nobody would want that out of you."

"You are correct."

After eating she wriggled just a little bit. Her hands wanted to keep exploring his body. But her mind was in the middle of painting.

Abraham reached over and crumpled up their trash. "Are you worried I'm gonna overstay my welcome?"

She denied it and he grinned. Then he did that thing with his face where his mouth was as still as ever, but his eyes were calculating everything. "Yep. I'm going. Can I get a kiss before I do, though?"

"Annoying that it has to stop at just one."

"Agreed. Very much agreed."

And with the promise of more smooching in the near future, he took off.

Chapter Nineteen

It made sense for them to ride with his brother to the bonfire. They were all starting in the same place, going to the same place, and coming back to the same place.

Unless one of them was on closing at the cafe, the brothers usually traveled together. So it would be irrational to shoot down Austin's assumption that the three of them would head over together. Even though he wouldn't have minded some alone time with Callie before her first beach bonfire with the group.

His brother launched right in with his charming patter before they got to the car. He relegated himself to the back seat and listened while Austin and Callie grilled each other about their lives. He knew a couple of her cadre of art folk, and they were deep into gossip about them before they turned on to Beach Drive.

It was fine. There was no reason to get touchy about it. The point of bonfire was for friends to get together. If Callie wanted to be friends with his brother, there was nothing wrong with that. So long as he also got to enjoy her friendship, which every indication said would be the case.

They arrived at the fire on the heels of Mateo and Alicia. Callie settled on the blanket between him and his sister, with Austin on his other side. He took a deep breath and pushed away his petulance, though Austin's smirk indicated he'd been less than perfect at hiding his emotions. Hopefully the brat would refrain from his usual commentary until they were alone in their apartment.

Of course, that was when Austin opened his orange backpack and gasped dramatically. "What's this?" He hefted a six-pack of seltzer. "You only brought a half dozen beers?"

Abraham twisted one of the sodas from the rings and handed it to Callie. "She likes these fruit sodas."

"Oh, give me one," Alicia said, so Abraham twisted another one out.

So much for Austin keeping his thoughts to himself. There was no chance now that he'd escape the teasing. And then Noah posted up, looking from the sodas to Austin and back to the sodas.

"Interesting."

"Isn't it just?" Austin replied in a sing-song, seemingly intent on deploying at least a dozen jokes at his brother's expense.

Then Noah looked up and patted the space on his own blanket between him and Austin. "Hey. Come sit by me. I want to hear all about how your project proposal went."

Leyla brightened as she sat, and Austin dropped whatever he was going to say in favor of watching closely how the woman of his dreams wrapped their cousin in a hug and kissed his cheek. It shouldn't have been such a relief to behold. But until Austin got around to believing he had a chance, there wasn't much Abraham could do about his little brother's eternally unrequited longing. Not much besides offer him a cold beer, which he did.

Mateo drew his attention, so he chucked him a beer, as

well. "Mr. Walters said he's going to email you about some contract work."

"Yeah? Thanks." The CPA had his office next door to James Family Bakers, and had long been a friend of Mateo's parents. Mr. and Mrs. James introduced them once Abraham finished his Business Accounting degree. For a while, he'd had his mind set on becoming a partner in Mr. Walters's small firm. But just as things had been lining up for that to move forward, his grandmother had died and left the three of them the funds they used to start up Pier Three.

Nick Walters still occasionally threw some business his way, which helped supplement his income from the coffee shop. Austin had the gig as building super, and the occasional contractor work. He didn't know if Alicia did anything to make more than the amount they paid themselves as Pier Three's owners. She'd cleared up her college loans during her stressful few years of corporate work, though, so maybe it wasn't such an issue.

The important thing was, they'd pulled together, gained a following in town, managed to offer a living wage and decent benefits to their employees, and still opted to meet up with each other and their friends around the bonfire most Friday nights.

It was more of a revelation than she expected to see Abraham relaxing around the bonfire with his family and friends. Something about the tension he'd carried on the ride over floated off to the ocean, even as he scowled at their teasing and put up a front of offense.

It wasn't just that she could sort out his genuine moods from his playing the part of the growly one. It was to do with the way he fit into the group so effortlessly, and was entirely at his ease with them.

Alicia canted her way to tell her they'd contacted their web designer about updating the Surfside Swell website to indicate which local businesses were Black- and minority-owned.

"Oh, already?"

"Yeah well. It's a brilliant idea. And also an obvious one. We should have done it from the beginning."

"I'm not sure how to parse something being both obvious and brilliant. I mean, something can be obviously brilliant. Like me, for example."

"Indeed you are," Alicia said, with that fond tone that meant she was fully on board with the sentiment, but also was teasing Callie a little bit about her habit of stating her own worth.

Callie stuck her tongue out. Her and Alicia's friendship dated back to when they were still clinging a bit to the vestiges of childhood, and sometimes they ended up a little immature around each other.

It was one of her treasures, that she had a friend who had been in her life so long, and knew her so well. And now she got to add Mateo to the pile of good in her life. It was easy to see why he and Alicia were so well-suited to each other. Their spirits were just so similar.

At one point, Alicia dragged her across the circle to meet Quinn, the web designer, and their boyfriend Jaxson. Quinn spouted off some things about SEO or SSL or who knows what that Callie could not begin to decipher. But Jaxson jumped in with a compliment about the recent photos she posted of her art, and launched in with language she could understand about the graphic he could layer atop the existing map to highlight businesses owned or run by people who identified as historically marginalized.

He was the draftsman who'd created the stylized town

map for the site in the first place, and she complimented his design in return. They launched into another of those 'who you know in Surfside' conversations that revealed how small town their tiny city really was. It turned out Salt was one of his neighbors, and they frequently dog-sat for each other.

"I didn't even know Salt had a dog," she said.

"You don't know Pepper?"

Alicia snorted. "Please tell me you're kidding."

"Nope. She's this adorably energetic mixed breed with a lot of poodle in her. She and my Benny are best friends." He pulled out his phone, and soon they were all doubled over laughing at the pictures of his large white wolf-looking dog sitting with his nose on his paws, while a scraggly grayish brown toy kind of pup climbed all over her. It was completely excellent.

Quinn launched into a story about when they'd taken the two dogs to the beach and Pepper launched herself into the waves. Every time Benny tried to follow, he danced away as soon as his paws got covered by the water. "We were laughing too hard to get video, but the memory is indelible."

Jaxson nodded. "You should come with us next time we take them out. Salt is always up for doggo play time."

After exchanging numbers, she wandered back to the other side of the fire and nestled in beside Abraham. He wrapped his arm around her. "Good?"

She nodded. "I like your friends."

"Yeah, they're solid."

"I didn't realize you'd set things in motion about the website."

"Of course. Why sit on a good idea?"

"Alicia called it brilliant."

"Are you fishing for more compliments? Because there's an entire vast ocean right there." He tipped his head towards the waves.

"Very funny."

He shrugged, which had the effect of drawing her closer. She relaxed into him. Leaning close, lips brushing her temple, he asked, "Do you want another soda?"

It was the most innocuous question on the beach, but his proximity made it intimate. She retaliated, whispering up into the shell of his ear, "Maybe a beer?"

He nipped at her lips, then tapped his brother's leg. "Hey. Give me a beer for Callie."

Austin lifted up from where he'd rested his head on the backpack. "One for you, too?"

"No, let me try the other one." Both his siblings stared at him. "I can't have a soda?"

Austin passed over the cans. "Seems like a banner day, when the 'coffee, water, and alcohol only' guy branches out. But you go wild, bro."

"You should spend less time talking." Abraham handed over the beer, then took several deep gulps of the soda.

She didn't miss his wince as he lowered the can. "If you want another beer?"

He shook his head. Gave her a squeeze. "It's cool. Got to try new things sometimes."

"Not like you drove here."

"No, but I ..." He trailed off, then flashed a smile at her. "Maybe I'm thinking ahead a little."

She bit her lip then buried her reaction in her drink. She wasn't sure quite what he was thinking, but she knew what she was. And it had everything to do with his assurance that these bonfires ended early, leaving the rest of the night stretching out before them, so they could do with it what they pleased.

Chapter Twenty

When they got back to the complex, he offered to take her back to his apartment. He didn't want her to feel she was always the one inviting him in. Or forced into accepting his new habit of showing up at her door uninvited.

Instead, she pulled him to a halt at her door, teasing him about avoiding what she posited would be the man cave of their place, and how she was sure it was full of nothing but dark furniture and bare walls and not a single throw pillow.

"I think that's because furniture makers tend to design for the comfort of an average male body, and average female bodies have to use throw pillows to make themselves comfortable. Then it just turned into a default gendered issue."

"So you and your brother never thought to have a couple of cushions laying around for the comfort of your female guests? Or your guests who aren't built along the lines of a generic male body? Which, by the way, is probably calculated from some skewed and biased Eurocentric study."

"Probably. And now I'll think better of our no-cushion lifestyle. You're the brilliant artist, so tell me: what goes best with our brown couch and blue armchair? Something yellow?"

She shut the door, sealing them into privacy, and shut his teasing, sealing her lips to his. He slid his hand into her hair, angling their heads so he could taste her at his leisure.

Something about kissing this woman was addictive. The more they kissed, the more he craved from her. When their lips separated too long, various internal alarms—emotional self-preservation, fear over disrupting the stability of his life, the risk of her brightness exposing his hidden darkness—began to blare at him. It only made him more determined to drown them out by kissing her longer.

He backed towards the sofa, Callie keeping pace with him as their mouths and hands explored each other's terrain. He was edging around the coffee table when a knock at the door startled him. He barely avoided landing on his ass on her floor.

Another knock, and his brother called out. "Abe? Callie? Come on."

They looked at each other. Abraham wouldn't be surprised if his frustration was as apparent in his expression as her disbelief was in hers. He shook his head, about to suggest ignoring it, when his phone went off. The knocking returned. He closed his eyes. He was going to have to see what the fucker wanted.

As he stomped to the door, his phone went silent. "What?"

"Our bathroom ceiling is dripping. I'm about to turn off the water main, and then I've got to see what's happening upstairs." Austin was toting his toolbox—a fancier grownup version of the one he'd gotten from Santa all those years ago.

He snagged his backpack and shouldered it on. "You need some help?"

"I can deal with the repair." Of course he could. He'd been learning the super's job basically all of his life. "I didn't want you caught unawares about the water shutoff. But yeah. Actually, can you go in and salvage what you can from our bathroom before it's all soaked?"

"Oh, sure, of course." His baby brother wasn't assigning him a pity task. Immediate damage control would make both their lives easier. He glanced in Callie's bathroom, to be sure the problem hadn't spread as far as her. Fortunately, her ceiling looked dry.

He turned to her. "You might want to fill a couple of water glasses real quick while you can."

She nodded. "Do you want me to come over and help? Make sure your decorative hand towels are safe?"

"No." He paused for a reorienting breath. Strove for a less curt tone. "It'll be a mess, but it's fine. My part of this is mostly mopping and laundry. Austin's the one who might end up with a real mess on his hands."

Callie wrapped an arm around his waist. She didn't mean it as sympathy for his uselessness, he was sure.

He leaned into her squeeze. "Okay. I don't know when the water is coming back on, which ... yeah. Probably means no getting filthy with you tonight. But are you still up for caving in the morning?"

"Oh, can this be an excuse for me to not go?"

Her grin broke through his moodiness. She was so fucking fun. "I'm not trying to force you into joining me. But I'm not taking this as an excuse for me to skip it, if that tells you anything."

She mock-pouted at him. "You are so obnoxious."

"Just you wait till I have you within reach of the bats before you go launching that accusation at me again."

She laughed, kissing his cheek before shutting the door on him.

His eyes were still half closed when he made it to the fridge in the morning to retrieve a cold water bottle.

"Oh, you are here."

He lowered the bottle and peered at Austin through crusty eyes. His brother slid the cereal and milk across the counter towards him. Abraham rested the cool bottle on his forehead, grunted his thanks.

"Did you finish all the plumbing last night?"

Austin's gaze dropped to the cereal. "Yeah, we talked about that when I got in."

"Oh. Right. I wasn't paying much attention." He glanced at the full recycling bin. After cleaning up the bathroom, he'd decided he may as well drink some beer while he waited for his brother. It made sense, what with not knowing how long their water would be out. Every time he grabbed a new can from the fridge, he looked at his neat row of reusable water bottles and nodded in appreciation of his sensible plan.

"It was a clogged toilet. I had to snake it. And if I tell you any more, neither of us is going to want our cereal."

He refilled the bottle and returned it to the fridge before helping himself to breakfast. "I appreciate your generosity to my delicate constitution."

Austin snickered. "If you want to be appreciative, try thanking me for covering for you with Callie earlier."

"What do you mean?"

"She came by maybe half an hour ago looking for you. I figured you'd headed out already so that's what I told her, instead of that you were still passed out from last night."

Callie. Caving.

Crap.

Chapter Twenty-One

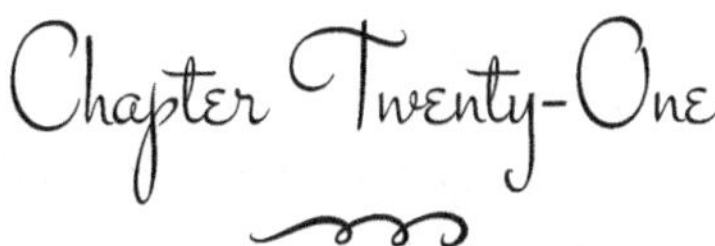

She wasn't a morning person. Never had to be. Probably another part of the unexamined privilege Alicia had talked about.

From the time she was accepted into the program at the fine arts high school, which sensibly didn't expect their students to do much of anything before nine a.m., she'd managed to avoid having to be anywhere or do anything before mid-morning.

Painting for a living afforded her plenty of days staying up as late as she needed. So, yeah, setting that morning's alarm only to be turned away at Abraham's door after she'd bothered to drag herself out of bed? And waited for what felt like hours before she went looking for him? Never mind that it was actually forty-five minutes.

It put her in a mood.

Nothing two or three of his cappuccinos couldn't fix, but since he apparently decided he'd be better off caving alone than either waiting for her, or making her drinks, it didn't seem like that was a pathway to salvaging her morning.

Did she think about not answering the door when he

eventually showed up? Yes, but she wasn't some asshole who made out like it was the make out Olympics and then fucked off without following through on his promises. So, she wiped her brush, and wiped her hands, and went to let him in.

She wasn't in the business of passing out credit to straight white men for basic decency. She might have awarded him half a point for his apologetic face and crinkly brow and beseeching eyes. But her business was art, not upholding the patriarchy.

So she didn't.

"Look what the bats dragged in."

"Callie." He moved like he would embrace her, which was a full-on mistake on his part.

She crossed her arms. "And a bright and beautiful good morning to you, too. How were the pseudoscorpions?"

"I'm sorry. I overslept, and Austin didn't realize I was home when you came by. We can go now?"

Ha. He sounded like that would actually work. She was learning more about his flawed way of moving through the world by the minute. "I'm busy."

Abraham looked past her at the easel and deflated a tiny bit.

She wasn't bullshitting. She'd been in a frenzy of work since realizing she was on her own that morning. Sometimes, working when she was tired could put a damper on her inner critic and fuel her production. Before, she'd only ever tried that from the staying up too late side of things.

She hadn't needed to learn it was possible to be productive if she got too early a start on her day.

"Do you want me to come back later for us to go out?"

She rewarded that nonsense with her most skeptical look. "When you're all suited up with your camping backpack?" She hadn't missed that he was kitted out and ready to go, wearing the same clothes from when he came from the caves the day she painted him.

If he'd dressed that way hoping to elicit friendly thoughts from her, he was out of luck. She wasn't inclined to revisit the early sense of promise she'd encountered that day.

So, no. He could damn well keep his second chance offers to himself. Apparently, his hopes weren't yet dashed, since he came up with another idea. "What about I bring you some lunch later?"

Her stare down was epic if she did say so herself. "What about if you just go crawl off to your cave and leave me to it? I don't want to be a jerk here, but I do have a deadline and there's only so much time I can spend messing around when I need to get this done."

His face said he knew perfectly well who she thought was the jerk in their scenario, and wasn't about to argue with her opinion.

Again, not something he earned points for.

He stepped back out of that 'hoping for a hug' range and lifted his hand in some sort of half placating, half farewell gesture. "I am sorry, Callie. For what it's worth, I wouldn't let this happen again. It was thoughtless of me to not be respectful of your time."

"Bye, Abraham."

She went straight back to her easel and let the rest of the morning be fueled by her unwelcome disappointment that she wasn't in the process of spending a couple of hours letting him show her what cave popcorn was.

Although she'd vetoed the idea, he swung by Saturn's after leaving the Addax system and picked up one of their brie and pear on baguette toasted sandwiches, and also their buttermilk fried chicken salad. And even though it meant putting up with Austin actually making a video of him preparing the cappuccino—"Good for social media," his brother claimed, with the cheesiest smirk in his arsenal—he wasn't going back to the apartment without peace offerings.

Squirming into that drop-down room at the cave, head practically fully upside down, somehow managed to clear out the rest of his hangover and clarify how much more sincere he should have been with the morning's apology. He'd said the right things, because he was Katherine Wells's son. But he'd been fully rushing through the necessities in hopes of reversing the divide between him and Callie.

Good thing his parents hadn't wandered past while he was at it, or he'd still be listening to the lecture.

He heard conversation over the music popping through her apartment walls, so he hoped that was a sign he wouldn't be disruptive again. Alicia answered the door. She rolled her eyes at him and turned back towards the living room.

"Told you he was making it for you."

He followed her in, shooting her a look she seemed to understand even though her back was turned. "Austin just uploaded your secret recipe. Hashtag half shot of vanilla, hashtag dash of cloves. Now I can be the one to make it for Callie anytime she wants it."

He ignored his sister and approached Callie, who was perched at her easel.

"This is just a drop off. I'm not expecting you to let me stick around."

Her up and down scan of him reminded him all too much of the day she dragged him in and told him to pose without a drop of concern for whether it was convenient. Impersonal, not entirely approving.

He didn't want to have lost that much ground with her,

but if they could reset to that place and still move forward, he'd take it.

"Strip."

He had his shirt off and was toeing off his shoes before his sister's squeal penetrated. "You are not painting a nude of my brother while I'm sitting right here. Hell, you're not painting a nude of my brother regardless."

"I didn't say he had to be nude."

He turned to Alicia. "She's got a lot of work to do, so if this is what she needs, I'm doing it."

"No one in the world needs a nude painting of you to exist," Alicia said. And, sure, it wasn't his top choice. But Callie had made it clear that he'd entirely messed up her morning. If stripping for her would help get her back on schedule, okay.

"It's fine, I don't want his face in this one," Callie was telling Alicia. "I just want his ass."

He'd been about to peel off his socks. He stopped and turned toward her.

She raised her brows. "Problem?" Her challenging look, and the fact his sister was still in the room, did add up to a bit of a problem for his composure.

He shook his head anyway.

"Good." She tilted her chin at the Saturn's bag. "Maybe put that food in the fridge, though. It'll be a while before I want to stop to eat."

"Why are you torturing me?" Alicia whined.

"You've been around when I've painted from life before."

She had? Strange to think of his sister having this whole familiarity with the art world that was all so new to him. They'd always been fairly close, but the past months and brought forth a lot of revelations—some more distressing than others—about the life she'd lived between their childhood years and the ones since they started Pier Three.

There was a time when his big brother status meant he knew pretty much all of her problems and was able to help her solve them. Or at least support her, while she solved them herself.

He hadn't expected to lose that status when he'd chosen to go down south for college. He'd figured he would stay plenty connected to his family, even while his siblings stayed in Surfside for college and he was in Claremont.

Maybe he wasn't entirely wrong, but it was clear there was a lot he'd missed. And even more clear that she was perfectly happy to replace whatever support he'd provided with the love and friendship of Callie, and Mateo, and even Austin, who'd been the one who never left Surfside.

Which was fine. They were adults now, and they could have a relationship based on maturity and equality. He didn't need his siblings to turn to him for every little thing.

Matter of fact, the more adult and independent they were, the more time he could devote to other interests. Like, for example, posing for Callie whenever she needed him.

Noah teased about being her muse, but getting her past the setback of the fire was important. That Wolfgang guy made it clear that she needed to step up the pace. And he was the one who'd started off the gallery owner's visit to Surfside in a combative way. So, it was on him to be available whenever Callie needed him.

Whether that was to provide caffeine, or to horrify his sister with the existence of a revealing portrait.

Before he could get back to shedding his clothes, Alicia punched his shoulder. "Hey, are you seriously about to strip down in front of me?"

"Callie asked," he said, like he didn't know that was going to make her launch her arms skyward.

"She didn't mean it."

They both turned and looked at Callie, who was switching

out the small painting on her easel for larger blank canvas. "Didn't she?"

Callie didn't acknowledge them, just kept on with her organization.

"Okay, she did. But that doesn't mean you can't wait until I'm gone."

"So leave, then."

"You're ridiculous."

"Hey, I just came by to drop off a sandwich. Callie's the one who demanded to see my ass."

Alicia glared at him while Callie tossed a couple of sofa cushions to the floor in front of her easel. She also disappeared into the bedroom for a moment, returning with one of those blankets that looked homemade, crocheted or knitted or something.

"Turn your back, Alicia. Abraham, pants off. And briefs, or whatever you wear, too."

"Boxers."

"Good to know. Lose them, and sit there. Cross-legged should work, but I'll let you know. Face the wall, and you can spare your sister trauma by covering your bits with the blanket."

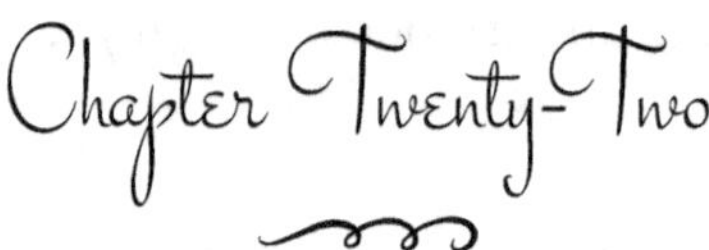

Chapter Twenty-Two

"Is this going to be for more wings?" he asked, settling down as instructed.

"Are you questioning my artistic intentions?" She shot Alicia a wink. Her friend bit her lip, like she could possibly hide how much Callie amused her.

Mostly, Callie'd instructed Abraham to pose to avenge herself after his mess up that morning. But as soon as she'd started telling him what to do, her well-honed artistic instincts took over and she knew just what she wanted from him. It all flowed on so well from the work she'd been doing that morning, and incorporated the exploration of permanence and transience she'd explicated while crafting her artist's statement for the solo show.

She stood behind her easel and regarded the expanse of Abraham's back. "Can you prop your left leg up and lean your elbow on it?"

He shifted, and she nodded. Then shook her head, and went around to kneel behind him. "I'm about to touch you."

"Mmmm." He drew it out all sexy and intent, and Alicia

made gagging noises until Abraham's back shook with laughter.

These two were going out of their way to mess with her. It served them right that she was going out of her way to mess with them right back.

With no more warning, she put her palms on Abe's scapulas and shifted the left one forward so it was a smooth curve from trapezius to oblique. She rotated the right so it jutted out from the deltoid, casting a shadow into the valley of his spine.

Abe grunted, but also stopped laughing with a quick hitch of his breath.

She was totally, absolutely, not noticing how his skin was so much warmer than the room, and held an earthy smell that combined enticingly with his usual coffee and salt scents. Or the way his skin almost rippled in response to the way her hands stroked down the planes of his back.

If she let out the groan her body longed to express, Alicia would go from fake gagging to pelting her with balls of paper. At least that's how they've have acted back in school.

Right. She was only toying with Abe now because he'd toyed with her that morning, and now she was low on sleep but high on productivity. Which was a little bit to his credit, but not so much that she would actually let him know.

"Alicia, toss me that throw pillow?"

"Letting it live up to its name, huh?" he teased as she caught the projectile.

She smacked her palm real close to the intimate part of his lower back "I want to see if it suits my purpose for this to be propped under your right glute."

"You are not putting my brother's bare ass on my peony throw pillow!"

"Hush. You had your chance to take it to Mateo's when you moved. You left it here. So, I'm using it for what I need."

"You are the worst friend I have ever had."

"Love you, too." She tossed a kiss over her shoulder at Alicia, who buried her head in the matching pillow.

Meanwhile, Abraham had gone statute still. She realized her hand was planted on the glute in question. Very carefully not squeezing his ass, she slid the pillow into place, then scooted back to evaluate. It worked.

"Comfortable?" she asked.

He cleared his throat, but nodded instead of answering. She cleared her own throat and managed to retreat to her easel without once glancing at the man's sister.

"Cool. I'm just gonna do some roughing in. Let me know if you need to, you know, move or anything."

He nodded again.

"You were about to tell me something about Mateo's sister?" she blurted to Alicia, once the silence had gone on so long it fucked with her concentration. "Maria?"

"Marina,"Alicia said. "Yeah, she's about to start her senior year at Surfside High."

"That's quite an age difference. Are they the only two kids?"

"Yep." She went on to tell her about the girl's summer job with Quinn, and how she'd called every company on the Surfside Swell site to collect voluntary information on the Black- and minority-owned status of each of them, and even gotten the names of a few other Black-owned businesses. She'd passed that on to Mateo so he could follow up with them about maybe being added to the consortium of locally owned businesses.

It was just the kind of chatter that she needed intermingling with her playlist to fill her mind with the perfect amount of noise so she could work without censoring herself. She didn't know if it was a full-on mind trick, or something to do with her upbringing, or what, but it made creating easier for her.

She knew it was one of the things her dad disagreed with her mom about on a cultural level. Her parents met when Mama moved from Portland to Ōsaka for her master's degree. Papa was the local guy she fell for. They ended up marrying in Japan and starting their careers there. Callie had been born in the same hospital as her father. It wasn't that unusual; so had a few of her cousins. But she'd always enjoyed their little natal connection.

When Mama landed the professorship at UC Berkeley, going to that hospital had been part of the Sayōnara Ōsaka tour she and Papa had made up. She didn't remember much else of it—she'd only been seven—but she remembered insisting that the hospital be part of their rounds.

And then they ended up in America for the rest of her life, which meant a lot of transition and stress settling in to a whole new all-English environment. Her American grandfather only spoke English, so she had a bit of conversational skill when she hit second grade at her Berkeley elementary school, but she had a lot of catching up to her new peers to do, linguistically.

Academically and artistically, she'd been set. Her mom's solution was to let her watch American shows in the afternoons while she did her homework and whatever art she worked on as soon as she'd raced through the school tasks. Papa acted fairly horrified by the practice, but Mama grew up doing the same thing and didn't think it would ruin Callie's brain. Since Callie liked her new freedom, and knew her parents disagreed about it, she made a point of excelling in school so Papa didn't have the evidence he needed to ban her TV time outright.

Besides, Papa was at work when Callie got home from school, and Mama arranged her teaching schedule to spend the afternoons with her. So Callie got all used to working with noise in the background, and also her English became flawless.

"You're not listening even a little bit, are you?"

She hummed an affirmative at Alicia, stepping back to take in the work she'd done on the new piece. "Something about understanding that your equity and access work has to be deliberately anti-racist, instead of just hoping that Black and marginalized people will seek you out because you're putting out nice vibes?"

Abraham coughed into his elbow. "Busted."

"I'm busted? You're the one who asked why BIPOC business owners wouldn't just notice the campaign and fill out the interest form to join in."

"Hey," he said, full of outrage and an unwelcome amount of twisting his neck to glare at his sister.

"Stop moving," she snapped, because their background noise conversation wasn't supposed to get in the way of her work.

But she couldn't stop herself from joining in when both siblings turned their laughing, fond faces her way.

Chapter Twenty-Three

Was sitting on the floor for hours with his ass out his ideal afternoon?

No.

Was simultaneously grossing out his sister and pleasing Callie worth it?

Absolutely.

Especially once he confirmed that the blanket she'd given him was bulky enough to hide everything going on under it when she put her hands all over him.

Even with Alicia sitting there, that had been so fucking intense. He was almost glad of her presence, because probably he and Callie should know each other a bit better before he started waving his erection around in her living room. It seemed only polite.

Though who was he kidding? Very few of his imaginings about stripping down in Callie's place were polite. He didn't know when she'd taken over his carnal mind quite so thoroughly. She'd gone from being someone he put up with living near despite the constant disruptive parade of creative people passing by, to someone whose happiness he would literally give the shirt off his back to achieve.

It didn't hurt that she seemed to find painting him a compelling activity. He didn't have Austin's cocksure vanity, especially after a couple of encounters with women who treated him like his missing limb make them more interesting for dating him.

He'd learned to look out for that kind of dehumanization and avoid it, but he'd never gotten together with someone who so obviously considered his left arm just another aspect of his anatomy, rather than something that reflected back somehow on the woman he dated.

If he was never again asked to give kudos to someone congratulating herself for seeing him as a whole man, he could finally give up stressing about the dating scene.

He knew Callie was only living in town because she needed a quick retreat after the fire, and likely she'd be bailing on Surfside as soon as she found a set up with a proper new studio, some place with all the things this apartment was lacking.

But he hoped to enjoy some mutually naked time with her before she moved on to somewhere better.

"Okay. There's officially nowhere to look now without seeing my brother's ass, so I'm hitting the road."

"I haven't even added any contouring yet."

"Trust me, the rough outline is more than enough." Alicia prodded Abraham with her foot. "I'm not telling our folks about this particular painting. I don't want to have to stand beside them as they view it, like I did last time. Your weird fuzzy chest was enough of a display for me, thank you very much."

"You've seen my chest before."

"Why do you think I'm always encouraging you to wear a rash guard? I'm trying to spare everybody on the beach."

"Shouldn't you be gone already? How long does it take to walk from here to the door? Cause if you need, I can get up and escort you out."

"God no."

He shot her glare. "In that case, maybe you could walk away, Alicia."

"Yeah, go away. You're making my model squirm too much."

"I'm leaving. I may never come back." She kissed Callie's cheek.

"Text me later about visiting the tide pools?"

"Will do," Alicia agreed, then lowered her voice to say something that Abraham couldn't catch. It made Callie guffaw though, so it didn't take much guesswork to know he was the topic. He could borrow a bit of outrage about it, but it would probably lead to Alicia staying longer. And he had no interest in that.

For a while once they were alone, he just sat and listened to her at work. It was interesting and unexpectedly soothing, the slight scraping and swishing noises just audible under the sound of her music.

But no amount of other input was enough to drown out the reminder that his inattention to basic inequalities meant he'd failed to protect and shepherd his community. So as he sat, bare assed and with unexpected free time to really think, he began to process how to make amends to those he'd neglected.

There was definitely something to this piece. She'd always kind of liked painting backs, and hadn't done much of it in her current series. It was worth exploring more for the future.

Because she had a huge future.

She could feel it. This sense of joy and rightness in what she was doing. It made her fingers tingle giddily to create. Hit her in almost a spiritual way, though she wasn't really a believer, despite her father's best efforts.

She stifled a laugh because it was all too ridiculous to be so philosophical and long range when really, she'd spent the past hour low-key obsessing about grabbing Abraham's ass again. It was a good ass, what could she say? She'd enjoyed groping it. Not to mention running her fingers down the ridges of his spine and across his graceful traps. So it kind of made sense to make plans for what she'd do when her hands weren't otherwise occupied by her brushes.

She was no doubt in a bit of trouble with this one. Probably it was Alicia's fault. If she hadn't spent years hearing the odd story praising Abraham's essential goodness and loyalty towards his family, she might be able to just paint him now, without also itching to yank the blanket away and explore the vibe between them.

She hoped he was up for a bit of exploration. So far, he seemed interested, but also like he probably wouldn't turn into a barnacle when it came time for her to move on. She'd taken Alicia's apartment for three months—just enough time to prepare and attend Wolf's show before she figured out where her next permanent spot would be.

Her place in Monterey would be fixed by then, but she'd already begun playing with ideas for other places to live. She had a fairly thorough list of what she needed in her working and living spaces. And a huge advantage in that she could take those requirements to any number of locations, and still do her job. So, if Monterey no longer suited, she would see where else in the whole wide world she could go.

Enough.

She would learn where to live later. At the moment, her concerns were a lot more immediate. She had a nice lean layer of paint covering her sketch of his form, but needed to do some playing before she could commit to the embellishments it needed.

She wiped down her brushes and dipped them in linseed oil before resting them on her drying rack, and took a new cloth from her pile to wipe down her own hands. Hoping they were now clean enough to be welcome on his skin, she knelt behind him, and leaned so her breath would feather across his nape. "I'm going to touch you again."

He tipped his head back to touch it lightly to hers. "About goddamn time, too."

She kissed his shoulder. "I'm sorry. It must have been uncomfortable."

He laughed. "Only as long as my sister was in the room."

She had the feeling he would never complain about the discomfort of posing, but she stroked firm hands across his back to help the muscles relax. "Do you want to put some pants on?"

That laugh seemed to startle him as much as his answer delighted her. "I have a few things I'd rather do in this state."

He dislodged the throw pillow and shifted so he ended up half reclined on the cushions. He cupped her nape and drew her down to meet his kiss. They kept the blanket over his groin, but he didn't seem concerned about if its placement was precarious or not. She kind of hoped it was, but wasn't quite bold enough to dislodge it while they were rolling around her living room and Sofia had plans to visit that afternoon.

But damn did she love kissing him. His face was just so yummy and intense and focused and good. The man had a good face. It was a face that didn't obviously invite you in, but the more you knew it, the more you could see how much nuance and intricacy it held.

Every kiss opened him up to her a tiny bit more, until it wasn't even that he was letting her explore his pretty much naked form that left her dizzy with desire. She wanted to learn every dip and line of his visage. To commit it to paper, but also see how his moods and modes changed it throughout the day.

To have not just his static image, but the constant pleasure of observing how his face reacted to the world around him. It was a ridiculous desire. Nothing she'd ever begun to contemplate before. But apparently that was the burden she'd accepted when she'd decided to kiss the guy.

His hand was toying with the hem of her shirt, and she super wanted to rip away all the barriers between them. Maybe she should forget about how overwhelmed she was and just drag him to her bed.

She was tugging him upright, and he was urging her torso over his, which made for some pretty mixed motions, but also sent all their hands wandering delightfully over each other's tense-teased forms.

He muttered some kind of admonishment to himself, but she was too busy growling in frustration to understand. Probably it was something about feeling desperate to get down to business, at least if he was thinking anything along the same lines she was.

But, because that was their luck, their delightful tussle came to a quick stop at a knock on the door. Abraham flopped onto his back. And Callie, because she was some kind of fucking hero, pulled the afghan higher to cover his pubic bone.

"I think it's Sofia, I was expecting her."

He groaned again, which didn't save them from another knock on the door.

She leaned down to kiss him. "I think you better actually put your pants on this time."

"Fuck," he said, and she couldn't have expressed it any better herself.

Chapter Twenty-Four

It was another full-on circus, and he was hiding in her bedroom like the surprise final act or something. See the amazing one-armed man trying to hide his erection! Goddamn joggers weren't doing much to conceal anything. And the mirror over her dresser gave away that even without the hard-on, Callie's posse would have a decent guess what he'd been up to.

Shame his hat was tucked into his backpack on her dining table. He ruffled at his hair, wondering if he should just spend however long her people were there hiding in her room.

The idea grew merit when one of them let out a long piercing whistle. "Salt, is this your ass? You didn't mention this."

"Excuse me, my ass is nowhere near that pale, as I'm sure Callie remembers," came the reply.

Callie's laugh was a sharp burst. "You're hardly that memorable, though I do admit you've got a lot of copper to you."

As the mirth and teasing ramped up, he opted to smooth the blanket over the bed and anchor himself there. His phone was also in his backpack, so he helped himself to the top book on the pile on the nightstand.

He wasn't fascinated by the subject of American Masters of the eighteenth century, but it gave him something to do besides eavesdrop, and wonder if he was making his eventual reveal worse by hiding out for so long. He hardly expected Callie to evict everyone, when she'd clearly invited them to start with.

He got that she'd liked people around. Maybe being an artist was such a solitary occupation that the visits were a way to cater to her sociable nature. Except when he'd seen her with the crowd before, she wasn't engaging with them. Same thing when he was posing today.

She'd asked a couple of questions to keep Alicia and him talking, but didn't try to hold up the conversation from her end at all. Which was fine. Most of the time he didn't like to chat while he was working, either.

Callie did seem to seek out the noise and busyness, even as she didn't contribute to it herself. He cocked his head. It seemed to be happening again—he heard a jumble of voices and activity, but none of them was Callie's rich, bright soprano. No doubt she was the diva in the room, but her arias were oil on canvas, rather than runs on a stage.

The soundtrack switched to something more indie acoustic than K-pop party. He sat up, feeling jarred even though it was exactly the kind of music that played at Pier Three all day.

It felt anachronistic to have it on at Callie's. Giving up on his appearance—at least his cock was under control—he headed into the living room. Callie was directing a frown at her speakers, catching Salt and Sofia in her crosshairs.

"Amity did it." Salt was pointing to where the woman with the teal hair was poised by a laptop. She was also about a foot from the bedroom door, which meant the whole room was watching as he pulled it shut behind him.

Amity tapped at the laptop and the music stopped. She didn't bother to start something new. Just what he wanted: a bunch of silence, and a bunch of people eyeing him speculatively while Callie went through the steps of setting aside her brushes, smiling at him all the while.

"Let's have that sandwich now. You want to split it?"

He closed his eyes, still uncomfortable being on display for her friends. But as much as she seemed to get off on teasing him, he didn't think she'd leave him adrift in their sea of faces.

"Now? Sure. You want the salad, too, or save that for later?"

She twisted her lips in consideration. He wanted to grin at how perfectly Callie an expression it was. Thoughtful and playful at the same time. Seemed like everything she did was irreverent, but also full of import. "It's not dressed already, right?"

He did grin then. "The salad? No, it's not dressed."

"Then yeah, let's keep it for later, when I can really savor it."

Goddam thin jogging pants. He headed to the kitchen to remove all the unruly parts of himself—his cock, his burning ears, the entirely lustful thoughts he couldn't suppress—from public consumption.

She put her own music back on before going to the table to wait for Abe to serve her.

Amity said something apologetic about her playlist, but she just shook her head and ignored the woman. Did she think Callie set up her environment to make it more of a party for her visitors? She'd specifically calculated what she needed, and definitely did not need a semi-friend from undergrad messing with it.

It had been tricky enough to set this apartment up in a functional way. She preferred to undertake the massive job of restructuring and recreating the gallery show without being impeded by some random woman's idea of what made for a nice workspace.

"That's a foreboding face you've got on," Abe said, setting the plate with half a sandwich in front of her.

She waited until he'd returned with a soda for her and his own plate before raising her eyebrow in challenge at him.

"I wasn't objecting. It's a little intimidating how sure you are all the time, but a little delightful too." He shrugged.

"I am a goddamn delight."

He snagged the water bottle from his backpack. "Cheers to that truth."

She focused on the delicious, if no longer warm, sandwich for a few moments while everything got back to some kind of normal in the room. "Thanks for this."

"If you haven't figured out by now, I'm all about the peace offerings."

"I figured it out. I like it."

"Well, that's good news."

"Is it? Are you the kind of person who's constantly needing to apologize?"

He shifted around a bit to see how closely her friends were listening. She thought about changing the subject to give him an out, but the thing was, she really wanted to know the answer. So, she waited for it.

He made another one of those faces of his that she'd begun cataloging and nodded slightly. "I do try to live my life thoughtfully, but I'm certainly not one of the perfect people."

"Are there perfect people? Where?"

He lowered his voice. "It's not perfection, really. I don't

believe that's a healthy goal. But I think it's possible to be more curious about how useful my life has been."

"I wouldn't say you're useless."

"No, but." He picked at the sandwich. "You've seen my flaws, at least some of them. Like, you saw how I failed to engage thoughtfully with the question of what we could do to help Black business owners. I didn't take the initiative to actively seek out the gaps in our planning, and only acted when a woman of color called us out."

"Hang on. I wasn't calling you out."

"I'm sorry, I probably sound like I'm doing some sort of performative self-flagellation. And that's messed up." He pushed back the plate. Took a breath. "I don't mean to stop you from doing what you want. Including chastise me. Don't worry that I've got a bunch of tender broken man feelings that need coddling."

Liam snickered. "Tender man feelings. Is that what you were doing in the bedroom? Exploring your tender man feelings?" He glanced back at the beginnings of her new painting, as if to make clear that he was referring to Abe's nudity.

It effectively quashed any of her own impulses to tease him about hiding out in her room. If she was making the same joke as Liam, she'd lost all semblance of her ability to judge humor.

Chapter Twenty-Five

"I'm out. Peace." He lowered his voice, encouraging her to join him in a little bubble of pseudo privacy. "Feel free to text me, or come by later, if you want to share that salad."

She pressed their lips together for a quick, decisive kiss. "Count on it."

It wasn't worth his while to pay attention to any of the other people in the room, so he grabbed his bag and headed away.

But the next person he saw wasn't Callie. It was Alicia, who'd gotten into his apartment somehow. Probably Austin, but his parents could be the culprits.

"What's up?"

"She's my best friend, you know."

He tried to not roll his eyes. "Are you warning me off or something?"

"No, I'm not warning you off. I just want you to remember that she's my best friend."

"What purpose is this notification supposed to serve? It isn't going to stop us from dating. Are you letting me know that she ranks higher than me, so if I break her heart, you'll break my neck?"

"Don't be an ass."

"Okay, then, don't be cryptic. You're the one with an agenda. Have you been lurking here for a couple of hours waiting for me to get home?"

"I have not. I just came down after Dad and I had lunch."

"Everything okay with him?" Even living in the same building, he never actually saw as much of his father as his siblings did. Austin because they worked together a bunch for Austin's gig as the building super. And Alicia because, well, probably because she and Dad liked each other a lot, so she made time to see him.

He didn't dislike his dad. Not even close. It was only that, going back to when Mom was the one taking Abraham to most of his occupational therapy and the prosthetist, and teaching him to manage things like medical claims and how to source adaptive clothing, it just kind of fell out that she was the parent he was closest to. And that the other two tended to go to Dad first.

"Okay, so you weren't lying in wait for me, but you're here to warn me of something?"

"Not warn."

"Because if you'll remember, Mateo is my friend, and I never barged into your apartment to tell you to stop sleeping with him."

"You're sleeping with Callie? You just met."

"Again, not your business. But no, you can relax."

"Good."

"For now." Her face was not amused. But his whole body was not amused about how she was in here griping about his choices. "I suggest you get over your random spate of possessiveness, or whatever this is."

"It's not possessiveness."

"It's not possessiveness. It's not a warning. It's not worry for her somehow fragile heart. You didn't barge in. So what's going on, Alicia? Do you have an explanation that makes sense?"

She was glaring daggers at him and he wasn't in the mood. Since she'd effectively trapped him in his entryway, he turned his back on her and started transferring towels from the dryer to the basket.

She muttered some kind of curse, but came up beside him. "Sorry. Look, you need a hand?"

"It's okay. I have one."

"Didn't you banish that joke for good when you were like eleven?"

"You were eleven. I was thirteen. More importantly, Austin was nine and thought he was super good at observational humor."

She snickered.

"Exactly. But now I'm an adult and can make what jokes I want in my own house, and also I can choose to not deal with my sibling saying shit at me in my own house." He turned in time to catch the wounded flash of her eyes, and the steam sank out of him.

Alicia's whole life, he'd always said for her to come to him if she had a problem and they'd sort it out. He'd never said what to do if her problem was with him, but there was no reason to lash out at her when she was acting on his express invitation. "I'm sorry. I like Callie. She seems pretty special to me, and she likes me. Maybe it's a go-nowhere kind of situation that will only last while she's here, and for as long as we're both interested. So, yeah, we're going to do some exploring of what that means for us. I'm not trying to upstage you, or cut you out. I'm not asking you to defend me or to put in a good word."

"I should hope not. What could I even be able to say?"

He shrugged. "One of my top two brothers."

She hmmed, skeptical. "Maybe on a good day."

"Well, let's hope she doesn't ask you to opine about me on one of my bad days."

"How about this? If you ever have a good day again, text me so I can gather positive evidence in case she asks."

He nodded, slamming the dryer shut. "Deal."

"Can you please let me help, since I showed up here uninvited and moody?" She wrestled the basket of clean towels from him. He hadn't suspected he and Austin owned so many towels until he'd needed them for cleaning up the bathroom leak.

He plopped down beside her, tugging a few of the wash cloths from the pile. Alicia started in on the bath towels, flicking them clear then folding and smoothing them with exasperating efficiency. "I care about your feelings, too," she muttered.

"Right back at you. Now can you maybe leave? I've been overdue for a shower since I got back from caving."

"Since you got back from bonfire, smells like. Now I'm questioning Callie's sensibilities."

"Ha ha. Very droll. Goodbye."

She gave him a hug, wrinkled her nose, slapped one of the freshly folded towels to his chest, and went away.

It was getting to the point that she couldn't contain her urge to get some. And the some she wanted to get was, specifically, from Abraham.

There was something beyond magnetic going on between them, and Callie was all for chasing down magnetism. Never mind how that chase went beyond her usual approach to her dating life. Maybe even because it went beyond her usual.

Whatever the key factor was, she didn't need to analyze it: she needed to do something about it. So, she did. Once everyone left, she cleaned up and knocked on his door.

"Who is it?"

She could *feel* him standing there, watching her through the peephole. Containing herself was its own kind of anticipatory torture. "It's the throw pillow inspector."

It must have been his head hitting the door that preceded his muffled laugh.

"Sir, this is not a laughing matter. We've had reports of a dearth of throw pillows at this address, and we really need to get it cleared up. I'm part of an official federal task force."

He pulled open the door. "I think I need to see some ID. People imitating Federal Throw Pillow Task Force employees is rampant, you know."

"Of course I know. My office—the FTPTF—takes it very seriously. We don't appreciate how some people just go around pretending to be part of the FTTFP—"

"FTPTF."

"Right, as I said, the FTPTF, like it's some sort of flirty game to them."

He nodded. "I can see how that would be extremely unwelcome."

"And it makes it hard for us to do our jobs properly. We're always having to allocate time and resources to tracking down leads about the imposters."

"That sounds exhausting. Probably you should come in and sit down. Catch your breath before you head out to the next investigation site."

"You, sir, are a generous citizen. I'll take you up on that. But what's this?" Hands on hips, she turned to him. "Mr. Wells. Has somebody absconded with your entire assemblage of throw pillows?"

He gnawed his lip. "Yes, ma'am, I'm afraid so. We fear it

was part of a coordinated heist from a gang of interstellar pillow pirates."

Seriously, fuck him for being too damn cute. She sidled up to him. "It seems I have no choice. The only way I can possibly be comfortable on your couch is if I sit in your lap."

"The difficulties you put up with."

Before she could respond to his silly, sexy tone, he clasped her to him. With one swift move, he tilted them over the arm of the couch so she ended up atop him, their bodies plastered together, and began to kiss the ever-loving hell out of her.

Chapter Twenty-Six

This. This was what he'd been craving. Callie in his arms, freshly washed hair flowing down over them both. Her lemon scent cutting into but never quite obscuring the tang of the paint smells that filled her apartment, even when she left the balcony door open for hours.

For once, he was clean and fresh smelling himself when they were together—no coffee, no bonfire, no cave sweat. He didn't know if she cared one way or the other, but it made him feel all the more ready for her that he'd use the afternoon to clean himself up and tidy the living room.

As usual, Austin's mess had spread across the place, but his brother had emptied the recycling and done the dishes that afternoon, sometime between surfing and his work shift, so it was fair enough. Abraham had even remade his bed, although wrestling with the damn fitted sheet was, as always, annoying. It was the one chore he regularly enlisted help for, as he'd sheepishly confessed on a message board once, only to have a flood of other people who used upper body prosthetics chime in to complain about the same thing. The general consensus was that help with anything larger than a twin bed was worth the sacrifice of independence.

He helped Austin with his fitted sheet in return. Fact was, making the bed was a pain in the ass, no matter how many hands you had.

Messing up the bed, though ... He'd take some help with that. He smoothed Callie's hair back over her shoulder. "If you're satisfied with your cushion investigation, any interest in finding out if I have throw pillows on my bed?"

She smirked. "I'm gonna go out on a limb and say no."

"Is that a joke about my congenital limb difference?"

"Uh-uh. But I can make a point of making some, if that would make you happy?"

"Only if I twist your arm though, right?"

She dropped her head to his shoulder. "You are definitely not as funny as you think you are."

He kind of was, though.

And he kind of knew it.

And she kind of was thrilled about the fact that they could tease and grope and kiss and laugh all at once. But also, that there was so much tenderness to the teasing. So much electricity to the groping.

Everything was so full of light and color, even though his bedroom was as predictively devoid of decoration as she'd suspected. The biggest surprise was the pleasantly green sheets, abstract and the color of bronze patina. The second biggest surprise was how organized it was. Though honestly after his succession of backpacks and rotation of reusable cups, she ought to have expected something along those lines.

As soon as they hit his mattress, something shifted. It was abrupt and thrilling. Whatever might have been romantic was now intent. Everything sweet became pure determined sensuality.

He shed his shirt, and for all that she'd spent considerable time with his bare torso already, it was still a revelation. All that skin on display for her enjoyment—for their enjoyment, because no question he was enjoying himself.

It wasn't just his erection that gave it away. He kept saying things like, "Callie, god, yes." And, "Fucking gorgeous." And, "Hell, yeah, please."

It was pretty good feedback, and she set about providing some of her own. "You should ... there! Yes, there. Oh god."

She covered her his hand with hers so he wouldn't consider moving it from her breast. Not that he seemed likely to do so, but hell, it was exciting. And then she got impatient and stripped off her own shirt. She hadn't bothered with a bra for the short trip down the hall.

Not when she'd been so very sure of her purpose. Abraham seemed pretty sure, too, as he propped himself over her and studied her body.

The silence stretched on and she was antsy to get them moving again. "Okay?"

"More than okay. A little overwhelmed with possibilities." His gaze traced upward to her face, and she was mesmerized by those deep eyes. "All good ones. There's so much about you I'm going to explore, Callie. So much I've been dreaming about."

Her brain was fizzing with sparklers. She took in—tried to take in—the meaning and the promise in his words. In his look. In the way their bodies pressed together, every little slide of skin and brush of breath an explosion.

She swallowed, not nervous, but akin to it.

Like this, being together, flesh to flesh, was so much more than sex.

And they hadn't even fucked yet.

He nodded, eyes a bit narrowed, and started in with dictates. "Don't move. I'm stripping us now."

Like she needed help sliding down her yoga pants. Like she wouldn't have enjoyed helping him out of his boxers. She ignored him and sat up to get her palms on his hips. It was important, urgent, that she hold him there. That she feel the warm skin she'd pretended to treat professionally while he was posing for her. That she inch closer and closer to the cock jutting towards her.

"You're moving."

"You're not," she countered. His smile. It had no right to slay her quite so fiercely.

Because he deserved to squirm for how he was making her feel, she scooted forward enough to taste that warm skin, nipping at the flesh over his hipbones, swirling her tongue around his navel. He was laughing, but his palm stroked her hair, smoothing the drying strands back. Which just made her back a bit damp and cool, so she jerked her head away and shook it fiercely, letting her wet locks lash his abdomen and, yeah, his crotch.

"You are such a devil woman." Abraham bent to wedge his shoulder into her stomach and wrapped his arm across her thigh, using the momentum to splay her onto her back against his pillows. He clamped his hand to her other thigh and pointed his left arm at her. "Try being still this time. I'm only asking for five minutes, and then you can get right back to torturing me."

Well, with a bargain like that on the table—or on the bed —who was she to complain? "Go grab my phone so I can set a timer."

He growled.

She licked her lips.

His palm tightened on her thigh. "Count in your head."

And then he set about ignoring any kind of protest she

came up with. Not that she could think of any, not with him bracketing her body and tracing down it with teeth and tongue. He'd gotten the message just right when they were both holding her breast earlier, and used the same delicious pressure to toy with her nipples. If she'd actually been counting, she'd have lost track somewhere between her left breast and the delicate skin just above her pubic hair.

How had she never known before the sweet torture of light-as-sin kisses to that line of not-quite-intimate flesh? His barely there brushes of barely damp lips, his gentle hums of reassurance while he rested his weight on her legs so she couldn't grind up against him. She squirmed. Her core was pulsing, and wet, and so goddamn empty, and Abraham hadn't even gotten to the good stuff yet.

She flexed her fingers, ready to bypass him and get there herself, and he must have sensed it. Or her desperation—probably he could sense her desperation. Because he sent her one piercing glance and that was it as far as warnings went before he ran the flat of his tongue up her slit and locked his mouth on her clit.

Her breath left her. It wasn't until he squeezed her ass, urging her to buck into his mouth, that she gasped and began breathing normally again. Or, normally for when she was about to explode. She was nothing but whines and pants and extremely focused motion. Her clit was swelling under his tongue, thousands of nerves bundling into one needy spot, and somehow her hands gripping his hair and her legs wrapped round his torso and her very soul sought ways to suction him to that place, to draw out the moment but also hurry it along because the next thing—the thing after the panting and the gripping and the whining and the gorgeous, gorgeous tension of it all—was when he took the gentlest, tiniest, scraping bite of her clit and she fucking exploded all over his mouth and his beard and his bed.

Chapter Twenty-Seven

Glorious.

She was utterly goddamn glorious.

Abraham rested his head on her stomach, reveling in the way her gasps caught in the air, and in her labored breaths undulating under his cheek.

One by one, she detached her limbs from around him from him, but left one hand idling through his hair. Eventually she went from stroking his hair to tapping the top of his head.

"That was fun, sweets, but I'm not done yet. You want to get up here?"

"Sweets?" He raised his head and licked his lips, enjoying the view of her body stretching up before him. If she thought his taking a moment to revel in how beautifully she'd come, to contemplate all the ways he would relish being inside her, meant he wasn't interested in more, she'd soon learn she was wrong.

Callie propped herself onto her elbows and looked down her nose at him. "You mind me calling you sweets?"

"Only thing I mind is every day since we met that I haven't

tasted you." He matched action to his words, nipping at her stomach, tracing his tongue along the underside of her breast. Once they were eye to eye, he brought his drenched fingers to his mouth and sucked her slickness from them.

"Oh, fuck," she whispered, pupils blown wide and cheeks flushed pink.

"That's the plan. If you'll have me."

"Abraham." His name was a benediction, and a challenge, and a plea.

He butterflied kisses across her cheeks and nose, ran his hand up her ribs. "You are stunning. I'm fucking honored to be here with you, Callie. And if you'll let me, I would very much like to show you some of the ways that honor is going to lead me to fuck you for as many hours as we can manage."

She shivered and grinned. "Promises, promises."

"They are. Can I?"

"If you've got a condom somewhere in this highly tidy room of yours, I suggest you find it now. Or sooner than now, if that's doable."

"I'll try my best." He rolled to his side and fumbled with his desk drawer until he'd extracted a condom.

She leaned over to snoop. "You have a little sex supply caddy!"

It was just a normal pencil organizer. He used it to stash condoms, lube, his cock rings and the remote for the vibrating one. He held up the condom. "Do you need a few minutes to marvel at my bedside drawer, or should we put this to use?"

"What kind is this? I've never seen it before."

"They're easy open, so I don't have to use my teeth to rip apart the foil. You can help yourself to a Trojan if you'd like to do the traditional honors, instead."

She was practically vibrating with curiosity, and maybe that would kill the mood some other time, but the little bounces she didn't contain sent her breasts swaying and somehow filled the room even more with the headiness of her arousal.

"No, I want to use this one. And, hey, your lube is water-based, excellent." She helped herself to it, and one of the rings. Her eyebrows played games at him. "Can I?"

"Knock yourself out. But maybe use that tie—the black one?—instead of the ring, since you've kept me hard for hours here? This you can wrap around my balls, too." He liked it because he could adjust the ring size one-handed, and never needed extra lube to remove it. And now he liked it because Callie bounced again when she pulled it from the tray and examined how it worked.

"Um, yes, I like this." Callie coated it with some lube and slithered onto his thighs, furrowing her forehead in concentration. It didn't do a damn thing to help flag his erection, but that was another advantage of the ties over the silicone rings. "Your dick is cute."

Damn the woman for making him laugh so much. He knew—knew to his bones—that she got off on teasing him, and wouldn't do so much of it if he weren't such a stoic grump much of the time. So, she said semi-outrageous things to throw him off his game, and expected him to respond with more gruffness. But then her eyes glinted while she teased him, and the right side of her mouth quirked up, and he just had to laugh.

He tweaked her nipple, and she yelped, and dipped to suck just the head of his cock, hard. His erection pulsed, and she snugged the tie's slider in close to the base. Good thing, too, because she was making him lose his goddamn mind, so he needed the assistance to delay his own orgasm.

Sitting up, he pulled himself back from her mouth and hands. But not before she managed to blow a cool stream of air across his wet cock, damn her again. "You're a menace."

"I'm extraordinary."

"You're an extraordinary menace." He looped his balls through the bottom section of the tie and trapped one loose end under his thigh so he could cinch the loop.

"Um, wow. That looks so hot." She traced the silicone trapping his testicles. "How does it feel?"

She was playing with his balls, which didn't equate to sensible conversation on his part. He grunted, then hissed when she squeezed.

"Good?"

"Condom," he demanded, and helped himself to some lube while she complied. His hand covered her whole pussy, possessive and intent, stroking the lube across her folds and dipping into her entrance. Since they were already kneeling on the bed facing each other, he urged her forward onto his lap and guided his shaft into her.

He might have lost it right then if he weren't using the tie. They were pressed so close together, her breasts sliding up his chest, his arms circling her back, their mouths back together in a celebration of the rightness of their joining. The pace was in her control, and she kept it shallow and slow. Each of her hums matched one of his groans, and it felt so fucking amazing.

So amazing.

"Abe." She made her way down his neck and across his collarbone in a series of small, urgent bites.

He hoped he knew what that meant. He slid his hand between them, and she looped her arms around his neck, and his thumb found her clit, rubbing and tapping in succession while her cries got higher and louder.

"Abraham."

It was a sound he'd never forget, the surging power of her calling his name while she came, grinding her pussy tight in his lap, laughter in her eyes and sweat across both their brows.

But he wasn't done with her.

He licked into her mouth, savoring the last of her inarticulate cries. He hummed a question at her, which she hummed back in affirmative, so he pushed up from his thighs to tumble her back onto the mattress. She barked out a sharp laugh as she bounced on the blanket. It turned into a sharp hiss when he palmed one breast and licked the other. It was a bliss he wanted to spend some time reveling in, but his cock was a rock and he needed to thrust.

Callie spread eagle, open to him in every way, and he was the luckiest damn guy in the galaxy. He braced on his left elbow and took his shaft in hand, lining them up and plunging into her with one long, satisfying stroke. The constriction around his base and balls seemed to make his blood rush like wildfire throughout his body—his head was almost spinning as he wedged his arm under her back to help arch her spine.

Loud as his heartbeat was, he still heard her demands. "There, that's it. Don't stop. Fuck. Harder, Abraham. What did you do? Did you just swivel? Fucking do that again right now."

He did. He did it again and again, everything ratcheting up with each withdrawal, tightening further with each thrust. Her body pulsed and pulled at him, and his spine tingled, and her moans made him even harder, made him more desperate to come.

Maybe she was still making demands. Maybe she was bucking wildly beneath him. All he knew was the rush and glory and grip and thrust as he buried his cock in Callie and rode out the incessant waves of his orgasm.

Chapter Twenty-Eight

She woke in Abraham's bed, which was strange enough to make her realize she'd finally gotten used to sleeping in the too cramped, badly lit, poorly ventilated one-bedroom she was subletting from Alicia. She never thought she got too attached to any particular place until she smashed up against the discomfort of waking somewhere new. It was a shame the sublet was so ill-suited in every way to her career, or she might start playing with the idea of keeping it once her crisis pressure period of painting ended.

Of course, it might be the endorphins of super sexy sex with the neighbor that had her wondering whether the lack of almost everything she needed in a painting environment was really such a problem.

She propped herself against the headboard and studied Abraham, comparing his resting features to those when he was surly, or joking, or exasperated, or relaxed with his friends. There was no tension in his jaw. It lengthened the lines of his face, and dented subtle hollows under his cheekbones.

He let out an adorable little sniffle and squinched opened his eyes. "You're still here."

"Well spotted, Mr. Obvious."

"Wasn't complaining." He scrubbed his hand over his face, and blinked rapidly. "Not complaining one bit. Good morning."

"Good morning."

"You have any plans for today? And if so, how much of them involve being in this bed for a long time?"

"Wow. What an original and captivating line."

"I thought since I've already picked you up, I could say whatever cheesy things I wanted."

She raised her brows, aiming for imperious despite how squirmy she felt with his fingers stroking over her bare arm. "Are you under the impression that I was so enchanted by fucking you that you can just give up on the subtleties now?"

"No, I was under the impression that I wasn't very subtle to start with."

"You make a good point. Carry on with your cheesiness." She couldn't stop toying with his beard. It was so soft, but when it brushed against her skin, it was so bristly.

"Give me two minutes and I will." He headed out, presumably to the bathroom. His closed door prevented her from hearing whatever he and his brother said, but Austin's chipper tone and Abraham's gruff one were clear enough.

She buried her head in his pillow to keep her giggles from carrying. Also, because it had that coffee-infused Abraham smell she was starting to like way too much. She grabbed a mint from his Drawer Full of Fun, crunching it so she'd be all set when he returned.

And to be even more set, she also grabbed a condom.

Later, catching their breath and sipping from the cold water bottles he'd carried in from the kitchen, he confessed, "My extremely annoying brother reminded me that I promised to help my mother with some bookkeeping this morning. I can put her off though, if you're free?"

"Since when does anybody sideline Katherine Wells?"

He sputtered around his water bottle. "Damn, I keep forgetting that you know my parents."

"Yeah, I was wondering—where you were when I was spending every Thanksgiving with them? I guess you had better things to do than hang out with your sister's college friends?"

"I doubt it was anything so memorable. I'd have preferred spending time with you."

She thumped the back of her hand against his chest. "I thought you were going to stop with the cheesy lines."

"You keep giving me openings. What am I supposed to do?" He swept his arm at her torso, as if to explain what he meant.

She had to sit up and glare at him. "Was that an innuendo?"

"Only if you want it to be."

"God you're awful. Lucky for me, I have something else to do today. Something besides the usual frantic creation, that is."

"Oh yeah?"

"Yeah, Wolf is gonna Zoom at eleven to take a look at what I've been doing. It's not ideal, obviously, with the lighting in the apartment, but hopefully it'll be enough to reassure him that I'll be ready by the time he needs photography. We're going to pull together everything already photographed and the new works, so hopefully it'll be a more comprehensive view then he'd had before."

"Speaking of comprehensive views ..." He made to lift the blanket.

"Okay. You are officially cut off. I don't want to hear one more cheesy line from you for at least a week."

He dropped a kiss on her shoulder and then sank back onto the mattress. "Harsh but fair. Unless this means you're not interested in seeing me at all for a week. If that's the case, I'm going to pout about the unfairness."

This time she was the one to lift the sheet. "Oh, I intend to see plenty of you."

"You are utterly rotten at playing fair."

"Live with it." She bounced up to collect her clothes. "Am I gonna run into your brother out there?"

"No. Fortunately, he only stuck around long enough to give me shit before heading to work."

"Good." She swooped in for one final kiss, then retreated to the doorway for her last comment. "Oh, by the way? You're cool if we don't tell Alicia about this, right?"

His *face*.

She tried her hardest to hold on to her serious and hopeful mask, but the struggle to react was just too much. She bent over laughing, barely ducking out of the way of the pillow he lobbed at the closing door.

In more traditional dating circumstances, if he wanted to see someone again, like he did with Callie, he might text her late in the day. It nixed the chance of getting together that evening, so he wasn't making room for overcommitment, but still gave him credit for good follow up. Of course, in other dating circumstances, he wouldn't be passing her door after finishing up with his mom, and wouldn't hear the chatter rising over BTS's first global number one.

He'd learned a lot about K-pop while sitting for her.

It didn't mean he was obligated to stop and knock on her door. Or to let himself in, when he suspected nobody could hear him over the noise. Or to react to her welcoming grin like it was an invitation to wrap her in his arms.

But these weren't normal dating circumstances. So he

wasn't going to second guess himself. Much. Especially because wrapping his arms around Callie meant kissing her birthmark, and looking over her shoulder at the canvas on her easel. Getting a chance to see, at least to his inexperienced and ignorant eye, something of what she was seeing and imagining when he was posing for her.

"You like?"

It took her prompting for Abraham to realize that he wasn't saying anything, and that the activity around them had petered out. The half-dozen other artists in the room fell silent to observe them.

He cleared his throat, hoping his exhale didn't sound too choked up. "I like it a lot. You're astounding. Is it ...? How are you ...?" He blew out his breath again and chuckled. "I can't begin to ask questions about it. There's so much I don't understand. But it's just so pretty. And I gotta say, kind of flattering, too."

She reached back and patted his ass. "Just painting what I see."

A couple of the others laughed, which was fair enough, because although he hadn't spent much time observing his own backside he didn't figure it was especially museum worthy.

Salt cleared his throat. "Hey, Abraham?"

He looked at him. "Yeah?"

"You might not want to sit down on your favorite chair until your pants dry?"

He twisted over his shoulder to see that, yep, Callie had left some blue and white fingerprints on his butt.

She circled behind him and snorted before resting her head on his spine, pressing a gentle kiss to his shoulder blade.

"You should get her to sign that," someone said. Liam, that was the guy. The one he wasn't exactly sold on. "A Callie

Hamasaki original. You could make some money off those chinos someday."

The way he sneered at 'chinos' was certainly a choice. Abraham thought about offering the guy a lecture on the costs of adaptive clothing and hacks for one-handed dressing. But if anybody wasn't worth it, it was Liam.

He settled for staring the man down while Callie offered up her cleaning solutions. Given the splattered state of most of her clothes—and that her entire wardrobe was only a month or so old—he wasn't quite sure how well her ideas would work. But having her fluster around his ass, and even more so, having her turn his ass into some sort of artistic masterpiece, he couldn't exactly mind.

It wasn't like her day needed brightening. She'd started with excellent sex and gone on to a nerve-settling meeting with Wolf, which even included a referral to a framer his curator recommended. She'd agreed to a good deal on framing her new canvases, so now she was spared the time that would otherwise had taken her.

Her afternoon had been energetic and productive and entertaining. So she'd hardly been pining for Abraham to walk in and offer up his broad chest for her to lean against. Or his compliments, or his reluctant amusement at the cobalt smears on his pants. But who was she to reject an offering of laughter dropped in her lap?

"You know what? You've got that spray bottle of rubbing alcohol for your prosthetic, right? Go take these off and spray the stains with it, and then put them in to soak. You can leave them in my sink, if you want, and I'll scrub at them later."

"You got it. But I'll use my sink. Any chance you want me

to come back here with some takeout in a couple of hours? Maybe once everybody's gone?"

She checked his expression to see if he was complaining, or hinting at getting them some alone time, or snarking about Liam and Salt and Amity and Amity's slightly tedious new partner whose name she kept forgetting. Instead, his face revealed an intriguing focus on what would happen once both of them removed their pants.

Now she wanted everyone to leave right away. She pressed a quick kiss to his warm, soft lips. "Is Kokoro still open? Because I used to love their renkon hasami-age. Oh, and the daikon salad."

"Yep. Any other requests? I'm partial to the sara udon myself."

"Perfect. You have your assignment. Come back around seven?" She braced her wrists on his shoulder so she wouldn't stain any more of his clothing. "Looking forward to it."

It was a good minute before they finished kissing and he headed out.

"I take it everything's going good there, yeah?" Salt asked. "Jaxson and Quinn told me they thought so."

"Why does everybody gossip about me all the time? Is it because I'm so amazing?"

"Oh, absolutely. Though, in this case I think they were gossiping about Abraham, not you."

She harrumphed like that was just too rude, but truth was, she kinda liked knowing that his community cared enough about Abraham and his happiness to go around gossiping about all the ways she was good enough for him.

Chapter Twenty-Nine

Next bonfire night, he was on closing at Pier Three, so it was his job to claim the fire pit.

He'd discovered that Callie liked licorice mint tea as much as she did vanilla oat milk cappuccinos, so he prepped a flask of that, as well as the ones of decaf—and the whiskey—Mateo had requested to pair with his biscotti.

He'd worn his prosthetic to work, and even though the TASKA hand could get wet—which was why he'd persevered through the insurance battle to get the thing; he couldn't serve as a barista and keep his terminal device totally dry—he never wanted to deal with keeping sand and salt water away from the delicate wrist socket. So, once he deposited the flasks and his backpack on a blanket, he headed back to the cafe to doff and stash his prosthetic.

Callie met him at Pier Three's back door. "Austin just dropped me off. He said could we grab some of the hazelnut creamer. And now I'm guessing from your smug big brother expression that hazelnut creamer has some kind of significance."

He smirked. "It means Leyla's on the way." But after a

long shift at work, he didn't want to dwell on his brother's hopeless infatuation. They slipped back into his office, trusting everyone else could get the bonfire underway while he and Callie generated a bit of heat of their own.

She reminded him about the creamer before he locked up. Good thing, because she'd spent a pleasurable few minutes scrambling all his synapses. He'd aimed to scramble hers in return, and the way she'd gripped his hair and panted his name suggested he'd managed. It was absolutely worth making a disaster of the papers on his desk.

Alicia was bent over the fire ring, probably hoping, again, to prove Mateo wrong about her log-stacking techniques. When she saw them approaching, arms wrapped around each other, she handed the wood to Mateo and jogged up to plant herself in front of them, hands on hips.

"How dare you sully my best friend. Don't you know Callie has to devote all of her creative energy to her art right now? How is she gonna make her well-deserved leap to international fame and fortune if she's spending all of her time managing your grumpy butt instead?"

"Maybe my grumpy butt is more exciting than international fame and fortune. Did that ever occur to you?"

"Bro, I've known your grumpy butt my entire goddamn life. I'm gonna have to say no, you are definitely not worth the sacrifice."

Noah came up behind them. "Who's making a sacrifice?"

Alicia nodded at Callie. "This one. And that one seems to think she won't mind that spending time with him will probably destroy all the sparks of creativity she's been cultivating her whole life."

Noah winced theatrically. "It's a damn shame. She had such a promising career. That's what they're gonna say."

"Yeah, at least for a week or two. And then she'll fade into obscurity, never to rise again. And it seems like no matter what

I say, my brother holds no remorse at depriving the world of her phenomenal talent."

"Well, at least you tried."

Alicia nodded, and then tried to sit between him and Callie. He glowered her away.

Putting up with his sister's verbal nonsense was one thing, but fact was, Callie's time really was precious. He wasn't going to waste a minute of it in not touching her.

Hell if it wasn't hilarious when Abe squirmed at all the jokes flying their way.

Maybe if the general vibe was that he was kind of a jerk, or a player, or otherwise a dodgy kind of guy, she'd react differently. As it was, the jokes weren't at his expense, or at hers, but were generally good natured and affectionate.

They were also more pointed than when they'd come to bonfire together before. Like with Alicia's ribbing, it was clear that everyone knew they'd progressed from the early stages of dating and into what she would call a relationship.

They hadn't talked about definitions. Or exclusivity. It hadn't seemed necessary: she was far too busy to date anyone else, and as for him? She didn't think Abraham would set out to date anyone else when he was as caught up in spending time with her as he seemed.

Plus, for all her teasing earlier, Alicia really would be looking out in that protective way she was beginning to realize was a family trait. But it had been a damn long time since she'd dated anyone enough to call him a boyfriend. She'd not expected to be overcome with the urge to pin Abraham down with labels.

That's what came of giving herself a modicum of space to contemplate this sort of thing. If she only focused on how busy she was, and how to squeeze in some time with Abraham despite the pressure, she could put off naming them until after she delivered her artwork to Wolf.

Squeeze. Ha.

Abe ducked his head to ask why she was laughing, but she was snickering too much to answer, and waved him off. He nuzzled her while his lips were all close to her neck, and she shivered. Lucky she had a whole flask of delish tea to warm her from the inside out, since he was working with the sea breeze to cover her with goosebumps.

Alicia unzipped her guitar case and started to strum. It wasn't a song she remembered from any of their campus roommate days, but it bopped. Austin stood, which he'd been doing off and on since they arrived, flitting from group to group. This time, he stopped in front of her, offering a hand up. "Wanna dance?"

She reached for him, even though it meant moving from Abe's body heat.

"Hey, don't you think Abe should dance with her?" That was Mateo, grinning over his cup of spiked coffee.

Like that, Austin reached out his other hand. "I totally do. Come on, bro. Show off your moves."

Abraham tensed beside her, but Callie wanted to dance. And she wanted to dance with him. As she hauled herself up, she kept hold of Abe's hand and tugged until he rose beside her.

Austin moved on to pull Noah and Sally into a loose circle, leaving the two of them facing each other over the blanket. She ran her fingers down his arm, walking backwards just outside the reach of the firelight.

Maybe she wasn't defining their status with each other, but she sure as hell recognized her own delight for what it was when he followed her.

"You know how you dance when you paint?"

"Mmm? I do?"

He moved closer, put his hand on her hip. "You do. Sometimes just a little sway, and sometimes you start shimmying your shoulders and I can't understand how you can do all your brushstrokes at the same time."

Delight, and something else. Something vibrant and high-intensity. Luminous, like the radiant yellow she'd use as an underpainting if she were to capture the sunset lingering on the ocean beyond them.

"You say the most adorable things."

He huffed and pulled her closer. "Next time I compliment you, I'm calling you adorable. See how you like it."

She tipped up to speak low and suggestive at him. "Remember how your dick liked it when I called it cute? If you don't want to lose out on moments like that in the future, I suggest you be real careful how you go about admiring my excellence."

An explosion of guffaws erupted behind her, and she realized Austin had overheard. With a growl, Abraham tackled him to the sand. For a full five minutes, they rolled around like damn childish brothers, all cracks of laughter and overblown threats and attempts to pin each other in place they seemed equally matched at evading.

Their sister packed away her guitar and approached her. "If I weren't so sure I'd have to excise the memory, I'd ask what set them off. I'm glad to see you still enjoy being an agent of chaos."

She slung an arm around Alicia and watched the nonsense show. "You know what? I really, really do."

Austin must have let her in. He wasn't even aware she'd returned from her dinner with Sofia.

She found him in his room, half-watching a movie and knocking back a couple of beers while he cleaned his prosthetic.

"Am I interrupting?"

"Hey. No." He rested his arm and the spray bottle on the towel on his bed. "How was dinner?"

"Good. We've been back a while, but I just brushed on a thick layer so I thought, you know what's better than watching paint dry?"

He grinned and kissed her, aiming at the last second for the tender skin of her neck, in case his breath was super boozy. She was palming his ass, so probably she didn't mind what kind of state he was in. "How long does it take paint to dry, then?"

"Oh, it depends on how fat the strokes are and what color it is."

"What color? How does that matter?"

She nuzzled into his chest. "I could explain all the chemical science behind why Mars black and cobalt blue are fast and lamp black and ultramarine are slow, but instead we could clear off that bed and get busy."

"Anybody ever tell you that you're a genius?"

She gave that little bounce that was like an outward manifestation of her happiness. "As if I mind hearing it again."

He turned to take in his bed. He hadn't wiped dry the socket or cleaned the hand. "Okay that's going to take a few minutes. As much as I appreciate the spontaneous vibe you've got going on here."

"Can't just sweep it all to the floor, huh?"

"Did you or did you not wipe down your brushes before you came over?"

"Point taken. Can I help?"

"Actually, maybe you can give me a few minutes and I'll meet you back at yours?" It would give him a chance to brush his teeth and also allow him to evade at least some of Austin's teasing.

She nodded. "Let me go get rid of Sofia then."

"You ... just left her there? What did you tell her?"

His eyes were probably wider than they should be, since she wrinkled her nose all cute and smug at him. "That I was gonna go make out with my guy. It's cool. We were talking about Eric Carle over dinner, and it gave her some inspiration for this children's book series she's illustrating. I left her absorbed with her notebook and marker pens."

"Why didn't she just go back to her place to work on it?" He couldn't fathom the desire to spend that much time in somebody else's space, especially when trying to concentrate. Then again, he didn't understand any of why Callie wanted so many people around while she worked. She was under so much pressure already. He got that she couldn't exactly spent eighteen hours a day painting, but all these visitors, and all her visits elsewhere, had to be disruptive to her goals.

She snuggled up to his chest. "Never mind what Sofia is thinking. We're adults; I don't mind admitting that I'm low-key obsessing on sex with you."

The stones weighing him down rolled away. "Low-key? Is that how you describe it?"

"Shut up and get ready to sex me." She leaned up for a kiss. "And please take three minutes to brush your teeth before you join me."

He scooped up his empties to drop in recycling as he walked her out, very carefully not stubbing his toes on the metaphorical rocks that lay all around him.

Sofia was already gone. She'd said she just needed another moment to finish up and would let herself out whenever. But it was more fun to tease Abraham about leaving her guests behind for a booty call than to explain.

Besides, he deserved a touch of torture. She'd gotten all excited about the idea of naked time with him, and he was four beers deep into his evening. Not that he owed her his sobriety, but she'd experienced how his half-drunk sloppiness made him less about her and more about getting himself off. She could make things about herself just fine without his help, especially once she'd used some of the insurance money to buy herself a few toys. If she was going to play with him, she wanted him to play with her in return.

Not just because the way he played with her when he was on his game was designed to leave her purring and content, but because it was more fun to get frisky with him if he was sharp. But mostly, yeah, the purring thing.

When he showed up thirty minutes later, freshly showered and entirely focused on her, she scarcely managed to rub the charcoal from her hands before hauling him into her bedroom. Whatever grumpiness had pumped the brakes on her libido when she'd fretted over how impaired he might be dissipated as he snagged her waistband and dragged down her leggings and panties. He didn't so much as nuzzle her cheek before swooping down to her core, using his tongue to separate her folds.

His hand went feather light, dusting the gentlest touches across her cheek and chin and shoulder and ear. It was just enough pressure to distract her, but not enough to arch into. Not enough to anchor herself while he lavished forceful attention on her labia and vulva. Soon enough, she knew, the wetness at her core came more from her body than from his tongue.

He narrowed his attention in on the aching sides of her clit. She clapped her hand around his left bicep, because he kept playing keep-away with his right hand. Not quite settling anywhere she could grasp it, leaving her to pull her own hair and mutter vengeful threats against him. It seemed like he didn't care at all if she followed through on them.

"I swear, Abraham, if you don't fuck me with your fingers right now, I'm never letting you fuck me with your cock again."

He just growled and let her writhe against the vibrations his throat sent all up and down her pussy. But then he did— finally—press the flat of his tongue against the head of her clit. She stretched her thigh over his shoulder, determined to give him as much access as possible.

Just when he gentled his tongue to aggravatingly shallow laps, he planted his palm on her breast. It was the first awareness she'd had that she still wore her shirt, and she let go of him long enough to rip it out of the way.

Abraham growled again and glanced up at her. "That's better." He lunged forward to suck one nipple, then the other, into his mouth, pausing to tickle each wet distended peak with his beard.

She pressed her aching core up at any part of his torso she could reach, tugging his own shirt high enough that she could at least press her folds against his skin.

She reached down to drag his pants and boxers down to his thighs, then leveraged up and flipped them so she was balanced on all fours above him. "You know, it's super rude that you haven't even kissed me yet."

He waggled his brows. "That wasn't kissing earlier?"

She pressed her crotch down so she could stroke herself up the shaft of his erection. A heartbeat later, he was cupping her head and dragging her down to meet his mouth. It was all toothpaste and her: a fresh-sexy combo that smothered all remaining discontent.

Reflexively, she arched her back and began grinding on his cock. Little circles that stroked the hood of her clit back and forth along his length. He dragged his hand down her spine and cupped her ass, playing two fingers in and out of her too-empty entrance until she was biting at his lips and moaning his name and rearing up to plant her hands on his pecs while she pressed hard and hard and hard against him, and came.

He could spend decades watching Callie orgasm against him. Her hands, his hand, his cock, a vibrator, his mouth—whatever she needed and desired to get her there, count him in.

If that meant being at her beck and call when her layers were drying, or casually evicting any number of her acolytes so they could make some noise in privacy, so be it.

Best possible way to spend his time, especially since his family had no more use for him. But, no. He was naming then interrupting those self-doubt thoughts, and focusing instead on how next to make the bright spark of joy grinning down at him come again.

"Since you're there, want to reach into my back pocket and grab the condom?"

She rotated enough to reach his pants, while he lifted his knees to give her access to pull them completely off him. The callouses on her hands as she ran them up his thighs made him shiver. He yanked off his t-shirt and bucked up enough to shove her duvet to the foot of the bed.

Then they were naked together, chest to chest, and the glints in her eyes pulled him deeper and deeper into his desire for her.

"It amazes me how patient you can seem when I know you're about to unlock beast mode all over me."

That's what he wanted: Callie to understand how his stillness was a surface thing over the fathoms of desire he held in check every time he was around her. "I'm here to amaze."

She scoffed, but didn't dispute it. Instead, she ripped open the condom and lifted herself enough to roll it down his aching cock. Of course she lingered, teasing his balls and toying with his shaft. Not enough grip, not fast enough, not enough attention to the head. But if she got off on torturing him, so be it. Anything that revved her up for the next orgasms he would earn from her.

Didn't stop him from growling her name, but she loved that.

As soon as she released him, he took over. Slicked his fingers over her entrance, determined that she would be ready and welcoming. Guided her hips up and over his cock, poised so she could lower herself at her own, deliberate, excruciating pace. As soon as he was sheathed within her, he braced his arm on her thigh, his hand on her shoulder, and pumped up into her while she rocked forward to the rhythm of his thrusts.

"Let me lick your fingers," he said, and sucked her first

two digits. Her hands tasted just faintly of the oil she used for cleaning. When they were slick, he tilted his chin towards where they were joined. "Rub yourself?"

She bit her bottom lip, and he rewarded her sauciness with a strong thrust. Before he'd withdrawn, Callie's fingers were pinching her clit. She tightened, then tightened more, and neither of them let up until she'd tipped over the edge.

He did not give her a break. Or himself. Like that, they shifted again, Callie kneeling and holding the headboard for balance while he thrust into her from behind. He loved the view of her peachy ass and of his cock disappearing into her folds over and over again. He loved bracing her with his left arm while reaching around for her clit, letting his fingers pinch and caress in time with the gentle slap of his balls. He loved when her inner muscles rippled around him again, and they moaned and cried out and came together.

Collapsing to the mattress as one, sweaty limbs entwined and restorative breaths filling the air, he was slightly afraid that what he really loved, was her.

Chapter Thirty-One

"Oh, shit."

He rolled over and found her staring at her phone. "What's wrong?"

"Shit shit double shit."

"Callie?"

She shook her head. "It's all my fault. But what a goddamn disaster. How could I have messed up this bad?"

Sitting up, he moved to read over her shoulder. She was out of bed and pulling on clothes already, though. "I've got to, I don't know what. What am I going to do?"

"Can you start by telling me what's wrong?"

She tugged up her leggings and dug her hands into her hair, groaning. "I had this piece at a co-op space. It's been there for months already and I shouldn't have taken that as meaning anything. I just thought they weren't very organized or popular, which is what I wanted to find out by placing it with them to start with. I should have got my act together after the fire, though."

"What happened to it?"

She was staring around the room like it would reveal some

hidden wellspring of calm. "What with everything, I just forgot. I meant to pull it, but it seemed low priority cause it'd been sitting there so long. But now they went and sold it. It's already delivered, and don't get me wrong: I'm never gonna mind a prompt payment. But I was counting on that piece anchoring the forest part of the show. And now it's gone. Shit. Fuck, this is a disaster."

"I'm sorry."

She sank onto the mattress and pulled her pillow over her head before screaming into it. "I can't believe I fucked up so much. I should have let them know to pull it as soon as I realized that I'd need it for Wolfgang. And I forgot. And then I remembered but forgot again. And I never got around to contacting them, and now ..." She dropped the pillow on her abdomen and pounded it. "Now I am fucked."

"Hey." His impulse was to offer a hug, but she was still taking her frustration out on the pillow. He collected himself and focused on the kinds of lessons he'd learned from his mother. "Okay. This sounds incredibly stressful. And like right now you're very naturally focused on how it's a problem, which doesn't give you much space to work on solutions. Is there anything I can do at this stage to make things better? Or would you rather vent and not talk about solutions?"

"Are you trying to manage me?"

"No, absolutely not, and I'm sorry I came across that way. That wasn't well done of me." He shifted so their shoulders touched. "I am also available if you want to switch from negative self-talk to venting about me, specifically. I'm totally ready to be the bad guy here. Or I can make you breakfast. Bring you cappuccino with a double shot of espresso? Run to the art store? Pick Liam up and bring him around for some cheerleading?"

"Ha. Hilarious."

"Tell lots of hilarious jokes, none of which will be cheesy?"

Abruptly she rolled over and flattened herself atop him. They were smashed together from chest to knees. "Nope, not good enough. Flip us over, I want you to fucking smother me."

He decided she wasn't being literal, at least about the last part, and hooked his arm around her back so he could roll them over. He arranged himself so he covered her, her head tucked just under his heart, and dropped gentle kisses along the part in her hair.

"This sucks," she moaned.

"It sounds like it really does. I'm sorry you're dealing with it."

"It sucks so much. I am the worst."

"I think if you check your records you'll find that you're the best."

She moaned again but didn't make any move to extract herself from beneath him. "Okay fine, I'm the best. Now, what the fuck am I gonna do about this?"

He was casting back to remember as much as he could about the things she'd said about setting up the show and the gallery layout. "You needed it to create the flow into the smaller room in the back?"

"Right, it was the transition to draw people from the winged series through to forest series."

He propped himself on his elbow so she could get a little more air now that she was talking instead of moaning. "Okay, and now you need a new threshold piece."

"Right."

"Congratulations on the sale, though. That's something."

She buried her head in his chest again. "Yes, it's amazing, I'm amazing. Hooray for me and my bank balance." She blew out a breath and wedged her hands against him, giving him a little shove.

He rolled off her and out of bed.

"Oh. Well, good morning."

He snorted and palmed his erection. "Ignore that. It's a natural consequence of getting my body close to yours. I'll get rid of it before I get your coffee. What do you want for breakfast?"

"You're really going to make me breakfast?"

"You've got to eat."

"God you're a sweetheart. Can you pick me up breakfast tacos when you go to get the coffee?"

"Absolutely. Egg, bacon, and avocado?"

"You know me so well already."

"I aim to please. I'll even remember the salsa verde." He finished pulling on his clothes, then opened his arms for a hug. "Text me if there's anything else, okay?"

She nodded, squeezing him in thanks.

His job now was to get out of her way. So, after one firm kiss, that's what he did.

She didn't know if she was going to make it. Everything had been lining up, everything had been under control. She'd even managed to play at having a relationship while still checking off tasks on the to-do list Alicia had helped her make.

She'd been skeptical about that, until her friend suggested gamifying it. She'd had Callie overpaint white on a discarded canvas board, then Alicia used permanent marker to jot down all the tasks—all except retrieving this one painting. When she finished a task, she painted over it, or drew a nice thick line across it. Never mind how reminiscent it was of a child's sticker chart; seeing all those brightly painted over tasks made her feel accomplished and calm about making the exhibition work.

Now she felt like she needed another whole tracking board

to figure out everything she'd have to do to make up for not pulling the forest floor painting from the co-op on time.

She needed more canvas.

She needed more Mars black. How could she have run out of Mars black?

But mostly she needed an actual good idea instead of the pile of half formed nonsense that greeted her with every page she turned in her notebooks.

"Hey. You've got this," Sofia said. Thank God her classes hadn't started back yet. She'd swung by mid-morning to help talk her through the situation.

"I don't know how you can think that."

"Probably from knowing you for a decade and seeing how you consistently figure it out."

"Not failing in the past is no guarantee of success in the future. Or the present. Probably it's one of those situations where I've used up all of my allotment of luck. And now I'm going to pull an Icarus, head diving straight into the rocky waters to my doom."

"Calm down, Pieter Bruegel the Elder."

"Purportedly."

"Okay calm down, purportedly Bruegel the Elder. You're not crashing into the sea. No one's writing poems about this particular moment in your life. Or what do I know—maybe they are. Maybe someday there's going to be a whole song cycle."

"The ballad of Hamasaki's small sublet. It'll be like the icebox plums and everybody will riff on it for decades to come." Callie tapped her irritation out on the cover of the notebook. But Sofia had, as usual, shaken up her perspective and given her a new way to approach her problems. "Okay, you're right."

"Obviously. Not sure why you doubted it."

"I wouldn't dare."

Sofia raised a single eyebrow so it cleared the oversized frames of her glasses. It was one of her signature 'waiting for the student to figure out she was right' moves.

"Still, the whole situation sucks." She tried opening the notebook at random, hoping whatever she'd sketch there would surprise her into inspiration. She was faced with a refinement of the quick study she'd done of Abraham's eyes his first day sitting for her. She started shading, because she hadn't quite got the ridge of his brow right.

"Are you going to put him in a forest piece?"

She scowled at his too-compelling face. "No, he's a distraction." She slammed the notebook shut again.

"Harsh."

"No, but it's true, isn't it? I'm spending all my time on pieces with Abraham. And when I'm not painting him, I'm hanging out with him. It can't be healthy, right? Spending every last second with him, either in reality or through my art?" She wanted to throw her pencil across the room, but it was her favorite General's 2B, so she refrained.

"You're the only one who can know that for sure," Sofia said. "Before this mistake with the co-op, were you on track with your show?"

She studied the previously delightful task list. "As on track as I could be, given that every damn thing I owned burned to a crisp a couple of months ago."

"So being with Abraham wasn't stopping you getting into Wolfgang Lewis's good graces?"

"Staying in them, more like. The only thing I could have done to make that man love me more was to have photographed the parasailing paintings before they went up in smoke. He doesn't normally deal in prints, but he really adored that series and would have printed a limited run on giclee if I'd had even somewhat usable shots of them."

"Shame."

"More Icarus falling than Phoenix rising, for sure."

"So now you're Hokusai?"

"Ah no, I'm not Hokusai, is my point." But thinking of the famous *Phoenix Glaring in All Directions*, all dark details and deep cadmium reds and oranges, and with Bruegel in mind, and the forest gallery she wanted to viewers to invite themselves into, she found a fresh page and began to sketch.

Chapter Thirty-Two

He was in the mood to cook, and they had a bunch of greens that needed dealing with, so he put together a charred kale frittata, and after a short-ish search, located the clamp for his cutting board so he could chop up a cantaloupe to accompany it. Callie claimed she'd be rid of the art crowd by seven, so he took a few secs to clean up his myo arm, and then himself, before toting dinner down to her.

"Beer? Water? Tea?" he asked as he used the cleared off portion of her kitchen counter to plate their meal.

"Hot tea, please."

He clicked on her electric kettle and shifted everything else to the table. When he joined her with the tea, she took it with a nod. "Thank you for this meal. It looks delicious."

"Of course. Well then, let's eat," he said, grinning a little as he realized he'd picked the phrase up from her. "Oh, hey. Austin wants to get started replacing our bathroom ceiling. I was hoping I could just count on showering and everything here for a few days, so I don't have to run up to my parents' place every time I need to avoid disrupting his work area."

"Abraham Augustus Wells, are you suddenly moving in with me?"

There went his damn ears feeling all prickly again. Happened way too often over the weeks since they'd gotten close. "Not permanently, just maybe for a couple of nights? I'm pretty much sleeping over here anyway."

She crinkled her nose at him. "Yeah, I noticed the subtle, subtle way you always end up near my door at night."

"Our doors are literally feet away from each other. If I'm in the building, I'm almost always near you."

"Yeah? Okay. That's a very believable excuse, which I totally buy."

"Thank you. I'll put a checkmark next to that one in the 'things I've tried that might work' column."

She popped a cube of melon into her mouth and didn't respond, though her eyes were dancing.

"Austin did hint that he wants to remodel the bathroom while he's got it ripped apart. Because heaven forbid he gets near a repair he can't turn into a project that'll use every one of his precious handyman skills. He's so excitable about that stuff, never mind that it could add on several days if he's doing it now. The original plan was that he'd wait and we'd use the bathroom in this unit once you moved out, and then once he remodeled our place, he gets to play at renovating this whole unit."

"Why are you always discounting his handyman work? It sounds useful and sensible to me. Doesn't renovation mean they can rent this apartment out for a bunch more than the pittance I'm paying Alicia now?"

He tried to not grumble. "I don't know about a bunch more."

"But more, right? He's improving the bottom line of your parents' business. I thought you'd appreciate that, Mr. Bookkeeper. You're kind of dismissive of him sometimes, you know. Is it because he didn't graduate college?"

"Crap, no. I don't care about that. Where did this come from? Did Alicia say that about me?"

She rolled her eyes. "Alicia and I have better things to discuss than your stuck-in-time relationship with your brother."

"We're not stuck in time. It's just that he was always so pumped about working with Dad or the super when he was little. The way he talks about handyman stuff hasn't changed since he was eight. Like, when Alicia said she wanted to turn this place over to you? It wasn't in bad shape when she moved in, but he'd planned on doing some fancy nonsense with your kitchen before we ended up evicting her from the Pier Three apartment so he could convert it. Which was another whole fun project for him."

She pointed her fork at him. "Stuck dynamic."

"Whatever." He didn't feel like investigating how true that might be. "Point is, she moved here before the kid had time to execute his plans, and then when she and Mateo shacked up, you needed a place. Austin was wild about getting you in here because he figured you'd make a disaster of it all, and he'd have an excuse to pull out his renovation binder and his power tools and do every single thing to it once you left."

She lifted her chin. "You mean all this time I could have been less careful about paint splatter?"

He ran his gaze over the carpet, furniture, and windows. Bit his cheek.

"Fine. You mean all this time, I could have skipped feeling guilty about paint splatters?"

He shrugged at her, shoving another bite of the eggs and garlicky yogurt topping into his mouth to stop himself from sniggering.

"God you people are the worst. And now you want unfettered access to my shower for days in a row? Brazen. But successful, I guess. Did Austin's plan to remodel later change just because of the leak upstairs? Is it too complicated for him to fix the ceiling now and stick with the original plan for after I move out?"

Suddenly, his grip on his fork was unhelpfully tight, and he was flexing and releasing his thigh muscles like they could carry him right past the awkwardness of everything he'd been not blurting out. He bit the inside of his cheek and flashed her a sheepish look. "Okay. So. We haven't talked about this, but I guess … I'm wondering if you might find yourself wanting to stay in Surfside? I mean, once you get the paintings delivered for your show?"

Callie sat back and simply looked at him. It wasn't a challenging look. Wasn't disgusted, or wary, or angry. Wasn't full of giddy glee, either. She didn't reveal any of her thoughts, other than by not revealing anything at all.

"I know this particular apartment isn't what you need long term. And you said the Monterey people were going to build something more commercial, which probably won't suit your needs anymore. So that's two places that aren't ideal for you to live. Maybe—if you want—I can help you look for something that's good for you, but isn't too far away for me?"

He still couldn't decipher her look.

It was tricky, aiming to reassure her while still being unsure himself if his scheme was a leap too far. But he tried. "It doesn't have to be for us to move in together. I know we're spending a lot of nights together now, but that's not—I'm not taking that as a carte blanche to jump into every room of your life."

"Hmm."

"No, honestly. I'm just thinking that since you gotta live somewhere, what about living here and seeing how it goes? Us spending more time dating and ... doing relationship stuff, if you'd like that."

She still wasn't saying anything, and now his throat was dry to the point of misery. Probably because of how quickly he was being forced to accept that all the things crowding his mind, as she got close to finishing her urgent work, were nowhere near the top of hers.

It was all too sobering, so he knocked back his beer. "Don't worry if you're not into it. Like I said, it was just an idea."

"An idea you've been discussing with your brother already?"

"We're not ... I mean, I wasn't making plans with him. I just knew what he was aiming to do with this unit once you go, and it struck me that if you're leaving here, maybe ..." He crushed his empty, because it had stopped being of any practical use to him. "I thought you might have been thinking about where you'll live next. And I wanted you to know my thoughts, too."

She nodded, just slightly, but still didn't say anything.

If he was drowning, he might as well go deep into his truth. "If you thought about staying somewhere close by. I'd really, really like that. But if that's not your thing, I get it."

Chapter Thirty-Three

"I'm going to MacDowell."

It wasn't part of any kind of plan for her to blurt it out like that. She wasn't even sure why she hadn't told him yet, or why she'd picked now to do so.

"You're going—sorry, I don't know where that is. Not a place in Surfside, right?"

She scooted from the table and tilted her head towards the couch. He took her up on the invitation, but didn't place himself too near her.

His leg was bouncing. She appreciated that he'd cast his heart out on the line for her, but now she had to navigate her way through the choppy waves of a conversation she'd rather delay until calmer days.

"No, it's in New Hampshire, actually. It's an artistic residency, I applied in the spring and got notified just before the fire that I got in."

"New Hampshire." His leg had gone still.

"It's a pretty big deal. Top of my CV, 'MacDowell Fellow Callie Hamasaki,' all that."

His nod was slow, but he didn't hesitate when he said, "Congratulations. I'm sure they're glad you applied."

"Sure, probably. I'm pretty great, as you know."

That slight exhale, she hoped, meant he was on board.

"I'm heading up there right after my show closes. It's a thirty-day residency, so it's not like I won't be back. I like basing myself in Northern California."

"Thirty days isn't so bad." He swallowed heavily, and shifted closer to her. "How does it work? A better space to paint in, I'm sure, but can you still blast your music all day?"

"All day and all night, if I want. I'll have a full studio, private accommodations, three meals a day, some of them with the other Fellows."

"Better service than you get with me. At most, I've only fed you twice a day."

His smile was so fleeting she nearly missed it. "Yeah, but I bet your cappuccinos are better than whatever they serve." He relaxed an inch or so at her teasing praise.

"Hopefully your fellow Fellows are as good at stopping by to offer praise and company as Sofia and Salt and all them. Even if they probably won't spend all their spare time fetching you primed canvases and so forth."

His attempt to tease, in her opinion, landed flat. She didn't go around forcing her friends to fetch stuff for her. If Sofia was the one who'd lost everything to a fire, Callie would have shown up with supplies for her, no question. "I already ordered everything I need to be shipped to Peterborough. No one has to loan me an easel or project lights for me to do what I need there."

"That's good. I mean, it's good you'll have such a great setup and can work however you need the whole month long. I'm happy for you, even though I'll miss you, for sure. But you're coming back after?"

She closed her eyes, because she could see his wheels

turning already. He was figuring out if they could find a place for her to live before MacDowell started, or if he should set up her housing situation for her while she was gone, and wondering if he should broach the idea of visiting her in her residency studio.

Instead of telling him that wasn't really allowed, or that it wasn't his job to go around fixing every imagined problem in her life, she dove into the main point.

She hadn't known it was any kind of main point she had to make, until this all came up, but it hit her with an eye-searing flash how much he needed to hear it.

How much she needed to say it.

"Abraham. Every time I say I'm pretty great, that's not arrogance, you know. Don't get me wrong: I definitely believe in owning my good traits, and not giving anyone, including myself, a chance to downplay them. But the fact is, my talent, and my ambition, are going to take me far. I don't just mean in fame, I mean, literally, it'll take me all over the world. Sometimes for residencies, sometimes for installations, sometimes as a visiting artist or lecturer. That stuff is already part of my life to some extent, and things like MacDowell, and my solo exhibition at The Wolfgang Lewis Gallery—it's just going to engender more of it."

She watched him for a reaction, to see if he was getting the scope of what she was talking about. He was shifting his jaw, a flush growing above his beard, and she turned sideways so she could cup his cheeks. Because maybe, if she just touched him, he'd open himself up to understanding.

"I feel like what you're imagining for us is a lovely little life, where we set ourselves up in some cute house here, one with large north-facing windows and excellent ventilation, and we spend most of our time in Surfside. Oh sure, maybe we'll go as far as Seattle or Los Angeles once in a while to see my paintings installed at museums. But we're not going to go spend a few weeks in Japan or a few months in New Zealand or a season in—I don't know. Where are there lots of caves you'd love to explore?"

He was blank for a sec, but cleared his throat and rallied. "Iceland. For the ice caves. I've been to Crystal Ice Cave up at Lava Beds, but the blue ice glacier cave on Skaftafell is a whole other level."

"Sure, whatever. Iceland. Point is, I don't have any idea what opportunities might come my way. But I know for damn sure that if—when—they do come, I'm taking them. Maybe I'm the kind of person who could manage decades in a sweet little house in Surfside with the occasional week or two of travel thrown in. It wouldn't destroy me." She smoothed back his hair, then raked through her own. "But, Abe, why should I settle for that, for not taking everything I earn that comes my way?"

"I didn't—"

"I'm not saying that we're so amazing together that it's a foregone conclusion. That either of us knows, or can begin to guess, if we want to spend decades making a life together. What I am saying is that if there's any possibility it would happen, you'd have to suck up and accept the fact that I'm ambitious. And my talents match my ambitions. So if the art world gives me new ways, new places, to pursue those talents and ambitions, I'm going to take them up on it. Maybe it's not a problem right now—this month, or even this year—but at some point? We have to grapple with the fact that I can't be happy if I'm pinned in place like some specimen. And I don't think you'd be content with a life of waiting around with a butterfly net, hoping I won't notice that what you're calling a home is really some kind of insectarium I have to struggle to escape from."

All the sudden he was a goddamn bug collector? What had he done besides hint she make Surfside her home base for a while?

He stood, retreating to the balcony door for a little space from her, and for the support of the ocean at his back. Catching himself clutching his left elbow, he shoved his hand in his pocket and blew out a breath.

"Callie. I already said it was just an idea we could explore if you wanted. I don't get how you jumped straight from that, to running off to New Hampshire ASAP, or to bouncing from there right across the entire globe. I never made a single move to trap you and keep you from going wherever you want. If this thing between us has an expiration date, fine." The remains of their meal sat on the little table like a sad still life of what was never again to be. "I didn't want that, which is why I brought it up. But it seems you do."

She perched on her knees on the sofa. "I don't."

"You don't have much time before you leave, though, do you? I guess the expiration was built in all along. I knew that. I did." He tipped his head against the cool glass of the sliding door. It was easier to look at the sketches she'd tacked to the walls, than at her. "I let myself forget, is all."

Fuck all this internal wavering between hot tension and numbness. His torso was one big cramp.

Not Callie's, though. She hitched herself onto the arm of the sofa, propping her legs on the coffee table while she bent her head to her knees. She mumbled something he couldn't decipher.

"What?"

She straightened some, and her whole face was pale. "I let myself forget, too."

He wouldn't—couldn't—move towards her. "What does that mean?"

"Look, I was being an asshole, talking so dismissively about a cute little house like that. I think part of me wanted to imagine it."

He grunted. So she had a nice vision of a life with him, so what? Her nice made-up future sure seemed to make her feel like he was trapping her.

"Not just for me, you know. I was imagining it for both of us."

The way she leaned towards him. Like she was hopeful that picturing herself unable to escape his evil clutches was somehow palliative. He pressed his shoulders into the door. "Just because I think you're fabulous doesn't mean I'm trying to trap you into some kind of stifling arrangement. I might be falling in love with you, Callie, but the way you leapt to the conclusion that I was going to never understand the kind of life you want to lead—the kind of life you deserve to lead— that fucking hurt, okay?"

"I didn't mean that—I'm not saying we're stuck going through life like that. I wasn't ... It's just."

So she had no reaction to the falling in love with her part.

That was fine; he could slide right on past it, too. "It's just what?"

She growled into her hands. "I'm not like you, okay?"

"Right, I heard you earlier. You're talented and ambitious and coveted and world-renowned. I get it. You've made that totally clear."

"That's not what I meant. The talent and everything, that's just a part of my work. It doesn't make me superior to you. I don't even—I mean, no, I guess I do believe in superiority. Because I sure as hell think that you're a better person than anybody else I've ever dated. You're ..." She waved her hand up and down at him, like that meant anything.

Yes, he did have a torso, if that's what she was pointing out. "I'm what?"

She blew out a breath. "Okay, so I'm not explaining this right, but my imagination? It's what fuels my work, you know? And I do all of these sketches, all of these studies, all of these starts and adjustments and refinements until I come up with something amazing. And then I work to perfect that."

He stood still. Not a move her way. "Are the others you've dated in this analogy the rejected canvases, and I'm the something you're trying to bring up to scratch?"

"Gah, Abraham. No. I'm just trying to articulate how my mind works. I imagine things, which is a skill I've honed. But only a fraction of what I imagine is good enough to turn into something amazing. The rest is fleeting, or inadequate, or not right for me. I won't know which it'll be if I don't take the time to play with it first. Dreaming about a house in Surfside, or an artist's residency in Aukland, those ideas are like the way I work. I imagine, and from there I create things that are beautiful, and meaningful for other people. I do the same with my life. Imagine the possibilities, then work to make them true and good. I have to. If I don't, I'm not capable of putting together a project proposal for MacDowell. Or of fucking getting past everything I own burning up, and still managing to make Wolf's show work. And I know that's not how you think. I know you calculate everything out to the nth decimal before you take a risk."

Look at her with the math talk. "Clearly I'm either bad at calculating, or more risk-taking than you think." Because, and this part he wouldn't say, if he was so lacking in imagination he'd never have pursued dating someone so far outside his own usual realm, much less suggested they work towards a life together.

Maybe, though, she read his thoughts with her super brilliant imaginative mind. "It's not like I'm saying you're completely hidebound and set in your ways. You do adventurous things, I know you do. It's just the way you approach them—approach life—that's so different to me. Like, you learn all about a cave system before you risk exploring it on your own. And then you, like, roost in your cave or wherever before you add any extra risks to your life. You evaluate how safe it'll be. You have to know exactly how you want things before you make them happen."

"As opposed to you, who throws around ideas and plans until you come across one that's going to work for you."

"Right, exactly." She pivoted off the end of the sofa and stepped towards him. "That's what I mean. I'm not someone who tries to predict or control where I'm going with my life. I'm open to every possibility, so I can grab on to the good ones when I see them."

If only hers was one of the balconies with a short drop to the ground, so he could escape over it. He couldn't back much further before she had him absolutely cornered. "Got it. We're just too different. Thanks for explaining it in such vivid terms."

She halted, poised like she would leap forward and recapture him.

He didn't wait for her to pounce.

"I added all this info to my balance sheet, and now I see that the risk of being in love with you is just too high."

He didn't bother to collect his dishes, or the shattered pieces of his heart, as he left.

Chapter Thirty-Five

He was afraid of the goddamn risk of being in love with her? What kind of bullshit was that?

If she was such a risk, why did he bother asking her out in the first place? Because it was totally his idea. He was the one who tried to lure her into the caves. And then when she didn't fall for that as a super romantic activity, he went and very specifically invited her to dinner.

He absolutely would not have done any of that if he hadn't run the numbers first.

She wasn't gonna apologize for calling him risk adverse. Facts were facts. It wasn't even an insult. If he thought one of his key skills was something she denigrated, then he wasn't giving her a whole lot of credit, was he? So that wasn't a sign of love.

She jabbed blob of hansa yellow with her palette knife and mixed it with the phthalo green, adding more and more until she was no longer working with the shade of Abraham's sheets.

Salt wandered up to watch her. "Is it—"

"Is it what?" She shouldn't snap, but how would he like it if she interrupted him mid-stroke?

"Sorry. I'm sure it won't dry as bilious as it goes on."

She shifted a few feet back, glaring first at Salt, then at her palette knife. Then at her painting. She'd fucked up the value and the saturation both, straying fields away from the dark, dense feel she needed for *Phoenix Falling Into the Forest*. The shafts and vanes of his feathers now were too light and too dull and, damnit, too bilious.

She was back to glaring at her palette knife when Salt handed her a clean wipe rag.

She snatched it away from him, and instead of thanking him like a person who understood the value of kindness, she hissed at him. "I'm capable of spotting my own mistakes, you know. And of cleaning them up once I do."

He held up both hands, like he had to goddamn manage her. "Callie, I'm not trying to do your job for you. You know I'm more of a critic than a creator anyway."

"Why do you say stuff like that? Are you looking for reassurance about your usefulness? Because I never asked anybody to help me with this show. Well, Sofia, but that's different."

"You're always welcome," Sofia said, which counted as almost a scold from her friend and mentor.

She shook her head quickly, hunching up her shoulders. "Fine. I'm being rude. You're all generous and good company. Unlike me. I just don't want everybody to think they have to crowd around cleaning my brushes for me."

Liam stepped out of the kitchen, drying his hands and looking guilty.

"Did anybody say they resented it? Or are you taking something else out on us, now that I stopped you from taking it out on your painting?" Salt asked. "And for the record, you should mix that green with some raw umber and white instead, to gray out the spines."

She looked back at the painting. He was obviously right. Not just because it would be a nod to the sea in Bruegel's *Icarus*, but also because it would set off the vivid cad red and draw the eye to the curve of her Phoenix's spine in his fruitless attempt to twist and soar away from the depths of the forest.

She shot her friend an apologetic nod. "You're right. That's perfect."

"Sometimes you're not the only brilliant one."

"I know," she snorted. "I have been increasingly made aware of that, thank you very much. My complete lack of superiority is crystal clear."

Sofia asked, mild and clear as always, "Do you think sharing the limelight means you can't be brilliant in your own right? Does it have to be something that only you get?"

"The wisdom of Sofia strikes again," Liam said, which was the kind of statement that went a long way to explaining why people valued the guy, even when he was constantly trying to be irritating.

"Okay," she said. "You win. Thank you for cleaning my brushes, and is that small round sable in there?"

"Coming right up."

As far as Callie could tell, he was genuinely cheerful about her demands. But his obedience reminded her to tap Sofia and Salt for help gathering the addresses of everyone in the Surfside art community who'd come together to help her manage the crisis of finishing up her show in record time. Once she had some breathing room—away from the task list, away from this apartment, away from every Wells she'd ever met—she would get around to being as gracious as she should be, and write thanks to them all.

Abraham dropped onto the sofa next to Austin, knowing it would jostle his game controller.

"Fuck you very kindly."

He watched as Austin guided his on-screen avatar to recover from the fall. "Do I keep our relationship stuck in patterns from childhood?"

"How was your day, Austin? Good job on signing the contract with the Whale Pod hosts, Austin. Did you hear that Scorch Madigan added a show in San Jose to his fall tour, Austin?"

He checked if his brother had the 'I'm bullshitting you' smirk on. "Wait, that's for real? Are tickets on sale yet?"

His brother scoffed. "I signed us both up for alerts."

"Damn. Thanks, good looking out. And good job on the podcast thing, too."

"See how I've learned all about being self-congratulatory from your girlfriend? Sign of growth there, right? If that's not proof we're not still little brats, I don't know what is." The avatar leaped for some digital treasure and sauntered through to the next level.

"She's not all that big on straight cis white men being self-congratulatory."

"Bummer. But, fair."

"Anyway, she's not my girlfriend."

"Because she refuses to commit to someone who treats his excellent baby brother like he's still nine?" Austin bumped their knees together. "Woman's got a lot of sense, you have to admit."

He didn't have to do anything of the sort. "Us breaking up had fuck-all to do with you."

The pirate robot dude on screen paused mid-step. "She broke up with you?"

"Jesus, thanks for the vote of confidence."

"Sorry. You've been going around smiling a bunch lately.

And not for nothing, drinking less. I kinda figured you were gone over Callie."

"I can be gone over her and still break up with her."

Austin stole his move of not saying anything, which just proved he was still a brat no matter what he claimed. He sat there, smug, saving his game, waiting and waiting and waiting until Abraham broke and spoke.

"I asked if she'd want to stick around Surfside once she finished work on the show. Maybe find a place that could work for us both, down the line. Which, by the way, the topic only came up when I asked if I could use her bathroom while you rip this one apart. So, I retract my fuck-all statement. It's all your fault."

Austin rummaged in their ottoman coffee table, emerging with the adaptive game controller and analog thumbstick. Abraham sighed and took them, closing his eyes against the whole fucking world until the audio cues informed him that his brother had loaded up the couch co-op they'd just bought. They nodded along to the music, spawned their characters, and let surviving the play-through together become their entire topic of conversation.

Just like brothers the world over who related to each other as adults.

Chapter Thirty-Six

"It's too late," Wolfgang said as soon as she picked up his call.

Her whole body went cold.

"Too late for us to come up with a new layout for the entire show so *Phoenix* can sit opposite the entrance."

She sprawled to the floor. "Wolf, you tease, you torturer, you treasure."

"You, my darling Callie Hamasaki, are the treasure. I can't wait to see *Phoenix* in person. It's gorgeous. So much depth, and such movement. I won't say you've outdone yourself, because I've seen the rest of the show, but this is going get people talking."

"Yeah?"

"Oh very much yeah. And get them bidding, too."

It was everything she needed to hear. She was at *that* stage. The one where she'd grown to loathe every line, every hue, and every ratio of the work. And every artistic impulse she'd ever had in her entire life.

She knew that meant she was close to the end. Soon, when she asked herself if there was any way that one more tweak could improve it, she'd be able to definitively answer in the negative. Before she got there, she always had the moment of loathing that left her feeling like she'd downed enough coffee to blur her vision and eradicate any sense of confidence in her technique. Or her subject. Or her general brilliance.

Ironic, since she'd not had a single sip of coffee in the days since Abraham smashed her equilibrium.

"Okay. I'm relieved. Tell me more about how it's going to be a success."

"Well, first of all, no question I would have used it for the calendars if I'd had it on time. And the postcards. But since I didn't, and since I suspect you wouldn't have painted a falling phoenix if the fire hadn't messed up all our plans, I'm going to grab hold of the next best thing and suggest we do a limited run of prints for *Phoenix*. And my assistant is already emailing a bunch of people off our list of modern art curators with a hint about wanting to snap this up before the competition starts."

Her heart was racing. It was everything she planned for, dreamed about, and committed to accomplishing for herself. And now it was sending blood pumping through her body like it was in frantic search of someone to share the good news with.

Tough luck, blood cells. No one else put much store in being around to celebrate her successes.

She slammed the door on that pattern of thought. It did her precisely zero amounts of good. Instead, she let Wolf talk at her about an increase in pricing structure, and a rush job run of some additional postcards featuring *Phoenix*, if she could find somebody fast to do the high-res photos they needed.

It was everything she coveted. She was like Icarus, but one who avoided soaring too close to the sun. Like a phoenix successfully sweeping out of the ashes.

She let it all wash over her, and pretended that the only thing she cared about was how well she could fly.

"You busy after this?" Austin asked Alicia as the three of them settled around the upstairs conference table.

"Not 'til later this afternoon. Somebody put me on the closing shift for today."

"You said you wanted to try new things," Austin cheesed at her, which was a cue for her and Abraham to exchange an 'our little brother is hopeless' look.

He caught himself, though, and was on the verge of disrupting the dynamic of him and Alicia treating Austin as the lesser of their equal partners, when the kid said, "Great. Cause we have to go beat up your best friend for breaking our brother's heart."

Now he wasn't exchanging looks with either of his siblings. He traced the grain of the conference table. It was a highly lacquered piece, originally custom made for a tech company that had shuttered during the recession. One of Austin's many local construction contacts had spotted it going for pennies on the dollar, and alerted him to it during the renovation and repurposing of their space.

"This really adds to the character up here," he said, interrupting Austin's hyperbolic recap of the past few days.

He didn't know exactly what the Grumpiest Gnasher grumbling in Grousingland was supposed to be, but he doubted it was an accurate representation of living with him.

Maybe he should take their mom's offer to move upstairs while Austin renovated the goddamn heartbreaking life-destroying soul-rending bath. If nothing else, it would mean he could consistently come and go from the building using the side entrance, which would significantly cut down on the odds that he'd run into Callie or one of her acolytes.

"Non sequitur much?" Alicia asked.

Austin pointed at their sister. "I think what Ms. Fancy Vocab here means is: why the fuck are you mentioning a table we've sat around more times than we can count on our collective five hands since I got it up here?"

"I noticed it was holding up well to all the use it's gotten. And the other day I was adding images to our site and saw it photographs really well. It's got these cool red-yellow undertones that pop nicely against the blue walls and ocean views."

Austin was the only person he knew who could look triumphant and concerned at the same time. He'd be impressed if the expression wasn't directed his way.

"Okay, now I want to talk about Alicia's best friend, and also about your—what did you call them, non sequiturs?"

"This is a goal setting meeting. We're supposed to be discussing the business and updating our ambitions. It's completely relevant to mention that Austin's work up here contributed a lot to our bottom line. Not just his brainstorm to create the Conference and Recording Suite, or all the contracts he's talked people into signing for it. But the work itself. It's really well done and I wanted to put that on the record."

"Is there somebody up here taking minutes?" Austin asked, pretending to search around, but his cheeks were flaming.

"Dude, take the win," Alicia said. "Who knows when he'll get all devastated again and start issuing more introspective compliments."

He ignored them. "Can you investigate what it would cost to install an elevator? I was thinking an external one up to the landing. It might mean redoing the staircase, but if it increases accessibility, I think it'll be worth it. I want to see how long it might be before we could afford it."

"Yeah, sure, I'll do some research." Alicia only a little bit sounded like she wanted to take his temperature.

Austin peered at him.

"What?" He narrowed his eyes right back at his brother.

"I'm just trying to draw the line between Callie breaking up with you and your focus on accessibility here." He glanced at Alicia. "I've got a couple of names you should contact, by the way."

"Great," she said. "Also, it's because Callie's the one who dinged him about inclusion and equity. And now that he's not got her to zero in on as a caretaking project, he's casting around for something new."

"Oooooh," Austin drew out the syllable. "That's also the whole deal about acknowledging my vital contributions to our bottom line. I knew all that color theory stuff came from her, but I didn't make the connection that his complimenting me was part of that thing he does to ensure everybody's getting their fair share of the credit."

He relaxed his jaw, forcing his grinding teeth apart. "I just think it's uncool to have an excellent space like this that's inaccessible to people with mobility issues. It's not to do with anything else. And it'll increase our revenue for more people to be able to get up here and pay us for use of the space."

"Did we argue about whether or not an elevator is a good idea? I don't think either of us shut you down, bro."

He ignored Austin, because it wasn't advancing any of their company goals to talk about who shut who down. Or about how Callie shut down his moment of emotional vulnerability, which he could tell Alicia was just itching to discuss. "If you two aren't prepared to go through our meeting agenda, I have other things to do today."

Austin pointed at Alicia. "Guess what color backpack is in his car right now?"

His sister leaned back and studied him like he was some portrait on the wall, and not an actual person who didn't need any artistic interpretation. "I'm gonna say green."

"Now, I can see why you'd say that," Austin said. "He clearly wants to hike far away from us, for as long a time as he can. But, know what else he wants to do?"

Alicia hummed and nodded. "Is it to wedge himself into a hard dark solitary place where nobody will come after him?"

Austin high-fived her. "Blue backpack for the caves."

He definitely did not need to stick around for any more of their bullshit.

Chapter Thirty-Seven

No matter how many times she got to the stage of packing her canvases up for transport, she sank into the same frantic last minute overwhelmed stress as she rushed to sort everything out.

Seemed like the only thing she'd entirely managed to do right in advance this time was to get high-res images and fill out her certificates of authenticity. Sofia had offered to print the documentation for her. She hadn't asked. It was Sofia's idea, and Callie had been sincere and generous with her thanks.

She had her canvases spread across every flat surface in the apartment, double checking the measurements for the framer. She was also doing a bunch of clips for a video to edit later for social media, about the process of preparing everything for the exhibition, when there was a knock at her door.

"This must be my amazing friend Sofia Petrova, who's been such a vital support to me here in Surfside as I threw myself into non-stop action to recover from the fire and prepare for my Wolfgang Lewis Gallery exhibition. She's a pretty amazing illustrator—I'm linking her site in the comments."

But when she pulled open the door it wasn't Sofia, it was Salt. "Everyone, this is Owen Salt. He's also a huge part of my artistic support system here in Surfside. And everywhere I've lived for a decade, really. We used to work in the same studio up on campus, with Sofia as our TA. Look for the link for Salt's site, too."

She clicked off the camera because, yes, Salt was standing there with bags of takeout. But behind him, holding a roll of bubble wrap and shouldering a tote bag of who knew what else, was Abraham.

Maybe Abe nudged Salt, or maybe he shifted forward on his own. Either way, suddenly her back was against the kitchen doorway and Salt and Abraham and Austin and Alicia and their dad all moved into the room.

She set her phone on the kitchen counter and crossed her arms, zeroing in only on Alicia. "Why are all the menfolk of your family traipsing into my apartment?"

Alicia just pulled her into a hug that started out smothering, but ended up uplifting. When they separated, she saw that Salt had left the food under the coffee table and was unpacking Abraham's tote bag. Tape, twine, a few pairs of scissors, markers and labels. Austin was already covering the smaller canvases with parchment paper, and Mr. Wells was standing over the dining table, staring down at the second painting of Abraham.

It was a beauty, one of her favorites. All hues of blue and pale yellow, with two magenta focal points at his scapulas where the wings emerged.

She was sick of looking at it.

She turned to Salt, who handed over a folder. "Sofia sent these with me. She'll come by later to help load everything out."

Later.

Later, she'd go through the certificates to triple-check them. Later, she'd ask Salt why he'd taken it upon himself to direct the Wells family in the proper wrapping of her art. Later, she'd sit in her suddenly and throughly empty apartment and wonder about the rest of her life.

First, though, she drew in a deep breath and turned to the three-dimensional Abraham who'd walked in and sucked all the space and air from the room.

He fumbled behind himself and slid open the door, retreating onto her balcony. He didn't ask, but hoped she would join him.

If she needed it, he would say his piece in front of everyone, and never mind his strong preference for privacy. Just asking Jaxson and Alicia to help him figure out what and when she might need some help had pushed him to the bounds of his comfort zone. Especially when he'd approached his dad to be part of the packing crew.

Fuck she was gorgeous. More vibrant than any one of her brilliantly compelling paintings. He'd fucking messed up bad.

It felt like ages before she stepped on to the balcony and slid the door shut. She crossed her arms and leaned against the opposite railing. Every cell in her body was a challenge she clearly didn't think he could match.

Which was fair enough. He probably couldn't. "I know I overstepped."

"Which instance of your frequent overstepping are you talking about?"

His eyes were so dry. He blinked. "Today's, to start out with. You didn't ask anyone for help, and I took it upon myself to bring all these people here. Salt said he knew everything you'd need for getting the art ready to transport up to San Francisco."

"He does. I was going to do it myself." She sounded so flat and contained. Like she'd never raised her voice in triumph a day in her life. He'd done that to her, and everything in him folded in on itself at the evidence that he'd misused the power she'd given him to hurt her.

"I know you were. Alicia told me. I know that's my fault for laying my bullshit about your friends on you."

She scoffed, which was fair enough. They weren't in a place where they could brush past his wrongs.

"I'm at fault in a bunch of ways. And my acknowledging them doesn't at all mean you have to give a shit, or respond in any way. Which you know, but I want you to know I understand that, too."

She hadn't moved from her perch. Callie being so still only emphasized the thousand wrongnesses of their situation. Same with her being the silent one, while he ran every word in the dictionary into the space between them.

"In case you cut me off before I get everything out, which, again: you don't own me the time to listen to my apology. But the biggest thing I need to say, is that I was wrong. Falling in love with you wasn't a risk, Callie. It was a blessing, and the very best thing my emotions have ever been used for."

He had to breathe for a sec. Get his voice under control so he could continue, since she wasn't stopping him. His arms ached with emptiness, but his lungs still worked, so he went on.

"I wish I knew if I still might have the option of following you to New Zealand, or helping you find a house with good light here in town, or even me standing in the same room with you ever again—if any of those are ever going to be happen. But if not, Callie? Every minute of being in your life has still been worth it to me, because those minutes gave me the impetus to get out of my own head. Or out of my own ass, as I'm sure my siblings would say. I'm not anywhere close to good enough for you, and probably never could be, but I'm a hell of a lot better a person now than I was before I met you. My love isn't enough to plaster over the things I did wrong, the unfair things I said. It's not something you have to accept or welcome into your life. But it's real, and I'm never going to regret it, and telling you so feels like the thing I most needed to do before you leave."

She didn't know which way to turn or how to break out of the shell that seemed to have encased her. It seemed vital to move, but also impossible.

Abraham squirmed a bit, across from her. He rubbed at his stump, just below the elbow, and shifted his jaw, and nodded. "I have more explicit apologies I should make. About snarking about your community, and about pushing you to discuss the future when you never wanted to, and," he squeezed his eyes shut, "about jumping head-first into defensive sarcasm when you were making a sincere effort to explain your position."

One tiny crack. That was all she sensed, the most subtle drift of fresh air across her cheek. She turned towards it, to face the Pacific, and suddenly felt a swirl of breeze lifting the hem of her shirt and sending her hair fluttering back over her shoulders.

She cleared her throat. "You're not a risk either."

When she looked his way, he'd crossed half the balcony, but held himself still at that point, just outside the span of her reach.

"I'm not?" His voice. So soft and so tentative and so very dear.

She shook her head.

"Because it's not worth fussing over me?"

The pure, aching hope when he asked nearly doubled her over. It suddenly was the easiest thing in the world to close the remaining distance between them. To palm his lovely warm cheeks and gaze into his deep, desperate eyes. To beam up at him with all the color and radiance and swift, bright bounciness she felt glowing out of her.

"Because loving you it the easiest thing I've ever done. And remember, I have enormous natural artistic talent, so I've done a ton or amazing things that have been easy for me."

"Callie. Fuck." He squeezed her tight to him. "You're perfect. You know you're perfect, right? And that I love you? Because, fuck, do I ever love you."

His lips crashed to hers, and she pressed herself higher and tighter into his arms. Gasping for a breath, she pulled back and thumbed the tears from his cheeks. "I love you, Abraham. And you're perfect, too."

Chapter Thirty-Eight

"Callie?" Salt poked his head onto the balcony. "Sorry. Liam's asking do you want him to trek up to the East Bay and borrow his sister's van to load up the pieces you have at your parents' house?"

She turned to lean back against Abraham's solid hold. "Can he promise me no toddlers will touch them?"

Salt relayed the message, nodded in response, and gave her the thumbs up. She glanced over her shoulder at Abe. "Liam's sister has twin little kids. He's the most indulgent uncle. I think he's volunteering so he has an excuse to hang out with them."

She felt the rumble of his skeptical growl under her shoulder blades.

"Okay, but think of it this way. With everyone here to help pack up, and Liam saving me the trip up to Berkeley, I'm going to have so much time to spare."

Abraham brushed back her hair and nuzzled her neck. "Stop trying to make me like Liam. I get this crew is part of the package with you, and I'm even gonna ask Salt and Sofia to bonfire, but there's a limit."

She laughed, and felt like she could float from the release of so much tension.

They were in love.

They were admitting they were in love.

She caught Alicia's eye though the glass. She'd been studying them, taking in Abraham's arms wrapped around her, and her leaning into him. As her friend smiled at her, she reached up and tapped at her heart. Callie returned the gesture, because, yeah. That said it all.

Abraham dropped his head to her ear again. "You think they'd mind if we snuck over to my place and left them to it?"

Ugh, she wanted to grind back against him. He always had to be so damn tempting. Instead, she moved her hand from her heart to his forearm and squeezed it. "It was your bright idea to bring along an audience to witness your big speech."

He groaned. "I forgot to thank you for coming out onto the balcony so I didn't have to say all that in front of them."

"You would have, though?"

He got that half-smile that said he knew she was wondering how to trick him into repeating his apologies and professions in front of his family and their friends. She pulled herself up to kiss the expression off his dear face.

If her sketchpads and charcoals weren't packed away in her bedroom ... ah, well. Even more incentive to finish up the packing party and empty her apartment.

"Come on. I need to film all this, and call Liam and my parents, and you have to go to your place to grab a cock ring and more lube, cause I'm out."

His bright eyes flashed from her to his family on the other side of the door. She managed not to shimmy her shoulders as she slid it open and hopped through it.

"Son."

Abraham turned, because he could tell Dad was addressing him, and not Austin. His father was still standing over the painting of his back, holding the roll of parchment paper but making no move to cover it.

"Thanks again for coming to help."

Dad hugged him tight. "I'm glad you asked me. Looks like it went well, your big speech?"

He blew out a long breath. "Yeah. It did. I need to spend some time really thinking about my own goals as we move forward, but. Yeah. I love her, Dad. And I think we've got a great future together."

"Proud of you. And I'm glad she loves you, too."

He furrowed his brow, 'cause he hadn't said that part out loud. It felt like something precious he was going to keep clasped to his chest.

Dad handed him the paper roll. "Tear me off some lengths of this so we can protect the painting. I don't want anything to happen to it in transit."

Austin butted in to add, "Must preserve Abraham's ass at all costs."

Dad scoffed. "If all you see when you look at this is Abe's butt, you need a class in art appreciation. Even aside from the fact that the wings are the same color as Abe's caving backpack, every knob of his spine is presented as something tender and precious. And there's the glow just here, under the wing that covers his heart. Look at how she echos that same glow in the lightest yellows where his neck curves."

The three of them stood there contemplating everything Dad said. Abraham blinked all the moisture back, because he wasn't gonna let a tear fall and mar Callie's work.

"Simon Wells, you big softie," Callie approached and hugged his dad. "I didn't know you were such a connoisseur."

"Well," Dad grinned. "When my daughter started bringing

a budding famous artist round to use my washing machine, I decided to educate myself about modern art. Made it easier to brag about how I knew her when, you see?"

"Aw, Simon." She leaned up to kiss his cheek.

"Dad, are you deliberately performing for the camera?" Alicia asked. It was then he noticed she was wielding her cell phone, presumably having captured all of that searing emotion for posterity.

"Oh, that reminds me. If anyone minds being in footage from today, let me know so I can edit around you." Callie glanced sidelong at him, and he made a note to let her know just how unbothered he was about the prospect of being a bit character in the public story of her career.

Just so long as he was a major part of the private story of her life.

Austin took her keys as they finished loading up her van. "Dad is going to move his car out to the parking lot, and I'll put yours into the garage."

"I didn't even know there was a garage here."

"Just for Mom and Dad. And my surfboards. The rest of us are out here." Austin winked. "This is the one and only perk of hooking up with the owner's son, so enjoy it for the one night you get it."

Abraham lunged at him, but half-heartedly. Alicia shoved them apart. "Being the middle child is the biggest chore."

Her brothers smushed her into a hug, which broke apart fast. Possibly because Alicia tickled them. She grabbed her BFF and gave her a hug that didn't hold a bit of her siblings' menace. "Thank you for helping today. All of you."

Because she was heroic, as well as superbly talented and blessed in her friendships, she didn't tell them all to please go away fast so she could finally get her hands on Abe's naked flesh. Her face might have conveyed the message, though, because Alicia said, "Yeah, yeah, we're the best," and nudged her towards Abraham. Austin told her he'd leave her keys in his brother's room, and they let her make quick work of the rest of her farewells.

And then.

And then!

It was, at last, just her and her love.

"Race you," he said, and took off before she even processed the words. She chased him down, reaching him just at the building entrance. He managed to get into the foyer before she laid hands on him, but then she pushed him back against the mailboxes and smushed herself against him. Laughing too hard, and panting just a little, she couldn't manage a proper kiss, so she butterflied pecks all over his cheeks and nose and mouth and neck.

Two or three people came in past them, but neither of them paid attention. Eventually they separated enough to regulate their breathing, foreheads pressed together. "I love you," Abe said, and Callie managed to not climb him like a tree and wrap her limbs around him right that second.

"You and your public declarations. Can you please, just this once, allow me a little privacy in which to express myself?"

He laughed, which was a sound the color of the clear blue sky, and took her hand as they walked back to her apartment. "I don't know if you noticed when I went to my place for a few minutes earlier?"

She tightened her hold on his. "I think we all noticed. Especially the part where you went straight to my bedroom when you returned."

"Hmph. I hoped everyone was too busy with lunch to catch that."

She locked them into her apartment and led him straight

to the bedroom under discussion. "Maybe they were. But I noticed. What did you do?"

"Only as instructed." He lifted the pillow on his side of the bed to reveal the lube and condoms and toys.

Gah, too fun. He was gonna blow her mind with how fun he always was, no matter how much he pretended not to be. "Strip."

The command made him collapse laughing to the bed, and she really had no choice but to pluck the sketchpad and a 2B charcoal from their crate and perch on the dresser while she captured the lines of his amused, sexy sprawl.

Until, that is, he did strip. As he bared himself to her, she dropped everything to watch. Nude, he approached her and showed off exactly how adept the grip on his prosthetic was as he peeled off her clothes. She shivered. His intent gaze, the warmth radiating from his skin as he pushed between her legs, the fresh-brewed scent that clung to him even out of his clothes.

"It's been so damn long."

It had. Maybe not in the linear sense, but in the piling up of lonely moments and the constant stabbing replays of what might have been. "I'm sorry I pushed you away."

"No." His tone was firm and flat.

"No?"

"I didn't consider the whole of your position, Callie. I pushed my agenda at you when you were balanced in the middle of the toughest period of your adult life. Of course you pushed back; it was the only way to keep yourself from falling."

"Abe."

"I'm going to be better at living for myself, instead of needing to feel useful to others to accept my own worth."

She wiped away a tear. "I love how much you give to others. Your heart is so tender and giving."

He growled, which made them both laugh.

Wrapping her in his arms, he brought them to the bed. "I'm not going to stop working to make things better in the world, that's not what I mean. But if I hadn't been scared of you not needing me—to pose, to bring you cappuccinos, to make a home for us, all of that—I hope I could have asked about our future without acting like all of my happiness rested on your decision."

She rolled them so he was over her. "I'm cracking up that we're having this conversation while your erection is throbbing away at me."

Abraham groaned. "Too. Fucking. Long."

"Aw, I wouldn't call it that. It's length is cute just as it is."

His shaking shoulders. Such beauty, the way they rounded to hold him up and shelter them both. But also, she guessed it was a little tricky for him to reach for a condom while he was so busy laughing. So, she slid her hand under the pillow and retrieved one. She left the toys.

Playing later, for sure. Because what the fuck was more fun than playing in bed with Abraham Wells? Nothing, that's what.

But more important than fun—more important than anything, just then—was for them to be as close and inter-twined and bare to each other as possible, skin and hearts and souls.

"Callie." He braced on his left forearm, lifting to give her access to cover him with the condom and guide him to her entrance.

"Abraham," she purred back. Sliding her hands to his ass to urge him forward. Tilting her chin while he thumbed a last tear from her cheek.

He sank fully into her, and they both groaned. The right-ness. The righteousness.

Thrusting, touching, teasing, togetherness. It wasn't but a

moment before he was coming at her wildly, telling her how perfect she was, telling her how much he'd missed her. Proclaiming his love with words, and actions, and sincerity.

And also with sexiness. Fuck if he didn't manage to one-handed lube up his fingers and find her clit, adding that extra touch of circling pressure to the thrill of his wild plunges and wicked withdrawals. He bit and kissed and tongued across her neck and shoulder and breast, sucking hard on her nipple and whispering brokenly, "Callie, love, Callie. I love you. Come for me, Callie, I need you to come for me, I need you. Love you. Yes, god, thank you, yes. Love."

And maybe more. She lost track of his words, and hers in return, as she shuddered and arched and pulsed high and keened higher and came, and came again, still, more, with him.

With the man she loved.

Abraham.

Epilogue

He thought, after helping out with hanging the installation, that he knew what to expect when he walked inside The Wolfgang Lewis Gallery for Callie's opening. At least visually—even if he couldn't quite persuade himself to believe in how glitter and flash the crowds would be. And *crowds* was the right word. He just about stopped himself from seeking out the placard listing the place's occupancy limit.

Mostly because: damn it was amazing to stand stock still and look at everything. The rooms were all brightness and color and energy and brilliance, and it wasn't because of the fancy attendees. It all came down to Callie's work.

Her paintings filled the room, even the white spaces, even the fucking ceiling somehow. Everyone moved through examining, and discussing, and gesticulating with plastic cups of wine, and pausing with hands over their hearts as they contemplated the work. He got it. He often paused in just that way to stare at what she'd created.

Wolf passed him, flashing the sheet of red 'sold' stickers. Already in the hour since the show opened, a few red dots had joined the one Callie had placed on *Cave Motherfly* during their final pre-show walkthrough.

"Don't worry, we're selling limited edition signed prints of it, too. I'll still make some money off your pretty torso," she'd said. "But I want to hang this in our home, so keep that in mind for your house-hunting while I'm at MacDowell."

He was the luckiest damn man.

Austin nudged up beside him. "Freaking out?"

"Awed."

"That's a pretty bold reaction to staring at your own butt."

He glanced at his brother, then clocked that they were near *Moonshine Flutters.* "You continue to be hilarious."

"I know. It's probably going to be really devastating to you when you realize how much pleasure you got from living with me."

He slung an arm around Austin. "Aw, you gonna miss me, little brother?"

"Not gonna miss having to live anywhere near that annoying ass of yours." He looked back at *Moonshine* and then squeaked. "Leyla."

Abraham grinned. "Looks like my fine ass has yet another fan."

Austin shoulder-checked him and moved to intercept Leyla, guiding her to a less skin-filled painting. Abe went in search of his increasingly famous and renowned girlfriend, and, after chatting with his parents and hers along the way, found her in front of *Phoenix.*

They'd been in a full-tilt rush over the past few days. Preparing the installation. Going over the logistics of her trip to New Hampshire and where they'd live when she came back. Her guest lecture to Sofia's class. Brainstorming with a nonprofit he'd found whose mission was to increase accessibility and diversity in outdoor recreation, and which was letting him rope Noah into acting as a hub for distribution of donated gear. They'd already approved his caving expedition proposal, and put him on the audit committee; in between everything else that was turning their days into whirlwinds, Callie kept teasing him about finding vast stores of new people to help out.

Turning their nights into whirlwinds of fucking. So much soul-soothing, mind-blowing, dirty-sweet fucking.

So it wasn't such a surprise, what with all the whirlwinds, that he hadn't had time to really examine her newest piece. He stilled to examine it. The forest filled most of the canvas, all browns and greens and touches of gold that seemed mysterious in some sections, and like a respite of cool shade in others. But small as the figure was, the man with elaborate red-orange-gold wings trying to stop himself from plunging into the forest depths was the absolute draw of the piece.

Callie slipped her hand into his, but went on talking art stuff with Sofia and some fancy people. He leaned closer to *Phoenix*. She'd said that Liam was the model, and he could see that in the long, sinuous lines of the body. But instead of the shock of pale brown hair and the bright blue eyes, Phoenix's face was covered in a dark, feathered beard below deep-set brown eyes. It wasn't entirely how she saw him—he'd seen enough of her studies to know that—but *Phoenix's* face was clearly modeled on his.

And something in the expression of his straining neck, and the way he'd tossed his head to the skies made him think that even if *Phoenix* didn't manage to soar away, the landing he'd make in the forest would be just the start of new adventures.

He must have squeezed her hand. She wrapped an arm around his waist, cutting everyone out of the intimate space between him, her, and the painting.

"You like it, right?"

"Of course I do. I'm still trying to master latte art, but even I can tell it's one of your best."

Her grin sparked and she whispered, "Wolf has three museums fighting over it."

"Can't say I'm surprised. I'm already looking forward to visiting it in situ."

She purred out a pleased sound, bouncing just a bit in the shelter of his arm. "And as long as we're together, so am I."

I've had the best time watching Callie dive beneath Abraham's grumpy, solitary surface, and I hope you've enjoyed getting to know them both.

Of course I'd love all the praise that Callie thinks I so richly deserve, but mostly (like Abraham) I value your time and your honestly. Please take a moment to review at any or all of the usual online spots.

The Pier Three Coffee Series wraps up with **Latte for Leyla**, wherein Austin, at long long (long) last gives in to Leyla's profound temptations. Excited? (He is.) You can pre-order it now.

Thanks for reading!

-Melanie

Acknowledgments

Each book of Pier Three Coffee has been super fun to write, but Callie! Oh, creating her was such total fun. Don't you think we should all be a lot more like Callie? (Unless of course we're already straight cis white men, in which case, be more like Abraham, please.)

I'm grateful to Dan Scott for art guidance (all errors mine) (errors are always mine). Also to my sensitivity reader editor, which, did I mention all errors are mine? Abraham is more of a dream to me now, thanks to your help.

As always, I'm grateful to Robert for being my soundboard and for editing help, and to my online writing communities, especially my fellow CRW board members and my #notwriting and IRP peers.

I'm super grateful to all of my readers. Twelve is my favorite number (I was born on 12-12) and my heart pitter-pats that I've had readers willing to accompany me across twelve entire published works. I hope you'll want to stick with me for dozens more!

About the Author

Melanie Greene lives in a tiny woodland cottage in a big skyscraper city, with her husband and kids and cat and dog and all the people inhabiting her imagination.

For more info, visit her at www.melaniegreene.com, where you can sign up for her newsletter to access new releases and bonus content. Also visit her at Facebook.com/MelGreeneBooks and Twitter.com/Daki_MelGreene.